About the Author

Born in England, Milan left for New Zealand in 1965. His pursuits in this remarkable land include tramping, cycling and exploring the great outdoors. He was inspired to write a book based on some experiences he had encountered, together with the fascinating historic, culture and development that shaped this land that he wishes to share with the readers.

Milan lives in New Zealand with his wife Veronica, his two adult children now married and with children of their own; all of whom support his endeavours.

AOTEAROA AN AMAZING ADVENTURE

MILAN HAUTLER

AOTEAROA AN AMAZING ADVENTURE

Vanguard Press

A CIP catalogue record for this title is
available from the British Library.

ISBN 978 1 80016 408 6

*Vanguard Press is an imprint of
Pegasus Elliot MacKenzie Publishers Ltd.*
www.pegasuspublishers.com

First Published in 2022

**Vanguard Press
Sheraton House Castle Park
Cambridge England**

Printed & Bound in Great Britain

Acknowledgements

Wikipedia
Google Maps
NZ History

Chapter 1
-34.504637,172.797441

The noise — deafening — shrieks and shouts. Oops, a chair just fell over, paper darts flying everywhere! Angela tripped over with a bucket of water, why did she have a bucket of water in the first place? Tiny Amelia fell into a draw of socks. As usual, Boston and Tyron were fighting in the corner and Paige shot a dried-up pea with a catapult that hit Olivia in the backside.

"Ouch, that really hurt, Paige!" bellowed Olivia.

Denise was playing tag with Peter, who slipped on the puddle of water and hit his head on a table. Simon couldn't be bothered with any of the ruckus; he sat alone, consuming someone's half-eaten beef burger.

"Here she comes," called Jon in a very loud whisper.

Not a sound, a deathly silence ensued.

"What is the meaning of this!"

Mrs Mayonnaise Spreadable the matron entered, her frizzy head of hair appeared to stand erect, her blotchy face red with anger. Just a stare from those lasered piercing eyes made everyone tremble. "Well, who is responsible for this?"

No one answered, all stared at the floor. In the stillness was a lone figure standing behind Matron, thumbing his nose, stretching his mouth and poking out his tongue. Aroha started giggling uncontrollably and wet her pants. Matron spun around and caught James attempting another facial disfigurement.

"What do you think you are doing, James?" exclaimed matron.

"Nothing, miss," replied James in a very uneasy manner.

"For that, my boy, it is solitary confinement for two days."

"Oh, miss," pleaded James.

"Go into the broken bones room right now," retorted Matron.

"Oh, please let him off," pleaded Aroha.

"Silence, girl!" Matron demanded. "As for the rest of you, I want this mess cleaned up. You will go without dinner tonight and you won't be going outside for two days. You will all read three books each and will be tested on all of them. And if anyone gets less than five out of ten marks, you will read another three books. And what are you boys doing here, anyway? When cleaned to my satisfaction, you boys go back to the boy's dormitory. I will be back in ten minutes and if this room is not sparkling clean and tidy, you can all expect more days inside, reading!"

Days went by, lots of reading and lots of tests but no outside activities and poor James locked in a room on his own; he began sobbing, wondering how Matron could be so cruel.

For twelve years, James lived in the orphanage from just a week old. He didn't know very much of the outside world. How he wished he could fly away like Batman, stories of whom he had read in comics.

Four days later, Matron let James out to join the other boys, the punishment had been extended a further two days. Aroha, one year his senior, went over to comfort him.

"You keep away from him," said Matron. "He deserved every minute and I have a good mind to send him back again." With that, she left the room in an almost regimental march.

James motioned to Aroha to sneak behind a book shelf. "I am going to run away. Will you come with me, Aroha?" asked James.

"I don't know, James," replied Aroha. "What if we get caught? Who knows what Matron will do!"

"I hate it here!" James uttered in a low voice.

"Me too," said Aroha, "but there is nothing we can do."

"Will you at least think about it?" asked James.

"OK," said Aroha.

And so, time passed by with James frequently being scolded by Matron for trivia. Aroha was yelled at as her bed was not neatly made.

"You kids annoy me so much!" growled Matron. "The creases on the sheets are a disgrace! You can make up all the beds for a week, and I don't want to see one crease!"

After tea that evening, Aroha met James in the hallway and whispered, "Yes, I am ready to leave but how can we get away?"

"Leave it to me," said James, "I'll work out a plan."

It was a warm Spring evening in mid-October and James crept into the girls' dormitory. The girls were startled by the presence of a boy in their 'Girls Only' area. James motioned to Aroha and she knew it was time. Discreetly, Aroha collected her few valuables and quietly slipped away without anyone noticing.

James had it all sorted; two large backpacks borrowed and full of stuff and food and he even managed to pack a pup tent in each backpack! Not to mention a towel and cake of soap each plus tooth brush and paste. Two bikes were waiting for them in the courtyard, hidden behind a brick wall.

"Not a sound," said James.

The big wooden door was still unlocked but as they opened it, the hinges screeched and creaked. They stood there motionless, listening for footsteps. None were heard so they gently opened the door further until they were both able to squeeze through. They tried to close the door as quietly as possible but the hinges screeched and creaked even louder. The door was closed and there was no one to be heard. Hurriedly, they crossed the courtyard and ran behind the brick wall. The bikes were waiting like friendly steeds, anxious to take their passengers up and away. With their helmets on, Aroha and James rode off as fast as they could. When they were a little distance from the orphanage, they stopped to evaluate their position.

"Where will we go?" asked James.

"Well," said Aroha, "while you were getting all the gear together these past few days, I have been working out a plan on this old map I found in one of the kitchen drawers. It's a map of New Zealand (Aotearoa)

I suggest we explore Aotearoa from top to bottom, what do you think, James?"

"Great," said James, "sounds like an adventure."

The orphanage was located at Cape Reinga with a campsite close by. Aroha suggested they pitch their tents at the campsite and start off early morning. It was a pleasant still night that allowed Aroha and James plenty of rest from their escape and travel the next day.

Cape Reinga, what an awesome spectacle this is where the Tasman Sea meets the Pacific Ocean. Māori history claims the pohutukawa tree is around eight hundred years old, located at the edge of the cape and that spirits of deceased Māori jump from the pohutukawa tree into the ocean to return to Hawaiki (place of origin).

For breakfast, Aroha and James had Weet-Bix which James borrowed from the kitchen, but they did not have any milk so they had to be satisfied with dry Weet-Bix. So dry that they were sure dust was floating out of their nostrils.

Looking over the map, Aroha suggested that they ride about twenty kilometres per day (not every day though) in order for them to get to Bluff, no later than early March before the cooler weather would start. James agreed. They packed up their tents and set off on their first excursion. They decided they would wash in the crystal-clear rivers they would arrive at. "You need to ensure good hygiene," said Aroha.

"I'm hungry," said James.

"You've only just had breakfast," Aroha replied.

"How much money do you have?" James asked.

They stopped at the side of the road and Aroha dug deep into her pockets. "I have $15, how much do you have?"

James rummaged around in his pockets; bits of sticky paper wrapping from who knows what, a marble, a nail, and $8 in small denomination coins.

"Well," said Aroha, "we will continue for a while until we get to a store and buy some provisions from there. I think our first stop for the day will be Te Paki, only about fifteen kilometres, and we can set up camp in a forestry area."

Well, it took an hour to get to Te Paki, but where was the grocery store! There was not a shop to be seen.

"I thought there would be something here," said Aroha.

"Oh, my stomach is rumbling something awful!" exclaimed James.

"Look!" said Aroha pointing to a direction sign to the Giant Te Paki Sand Dunes, and only three kilometres away. They pedalled onwards and soon reached the sand dunes.

"Wow! I've never seen dunes so high, about a hundred and fifty metres. Shall we slide down?" asked James.

"I think not," Aroha replied. "It would be a bit of a climb at a hundred and fifty metres and we haven't eaten very much. We should save our energy until we get to a food store which will be probably sometime tomorrow. But we can sit on the sand for a while and rest."

There was plenty of bread in the backpacks and two bottles of spring water each. Sitting on the warm sand, they ate a few slices each and watched the daring on their sandboards skimming down the gigantic dunes. What fun it seemed, an adrenalin rush to be sure!

After a good long rest, Aroha motioned it was time to be on their way. They biked the three kilometres back onto State Highway 1 and rode for a short while until they found a small area of trees off the road where they could set up camp. Fortunately, Aroha brought her favourite book with her, *The Famous Five — Five on a Treasure Island*. She often dreamed of exploring a desert island searching for hidden treasure. James kept his very private diary with entries several times a day.

Munching on more bread for dinner, they were both yearning for some real food like burgers and chips, stuff that's extra good for kids. "We'll need to have an early night," said Aroha, "we will be biking twice the distance we did today, some thirty kilometres to Te Kao. I think there is a local store at Te Kao where we can get some provisions."

"Sounds good," said James and they turned in for an early night.

That morning, a slight northerly breeze developed. "This will be good for biking," said Aroha, "the breeze will push us southward to Te Kao."

After another extremely dry Weet-Bix, they packed up.

"I have sun block in my bag," mentioned James, "we had better slip slop this on as we will be exposed to the sun for most of the day."

"Good idea," said Aroha. "Helmets on and let's go."

The rural scenery was just something else, a mob of sheep being driven into the yards, while another group were being released from being shorn. Dogs rounding up some strays and herding them in with the mob. Pukekos running in all directions in small pockets of swampy marshes. "Look!" said James. There was a kingfisher sitting on a power line gazing into the stream below, waiting for its lunch to swim by.

"I need to go for a wee," said James.

"OK," sighed Aroha, "you had better go behind that tree."

They stopped on the side of the road. Aroha took guard over the bikes while James went behind the tree. "I've finished," said James in a loud voice.

"Good, let's go," said Aroha. "At this rate, we will probably just make Te Kao by midnight."

The traffic was starting to pick up. Even though it was a State Highway, the road especially for cyclists was narrow in parts with very little room to manoeuvre. With vehicles passing at hundred kilometres per hour, you needed to stay focussed on keeping within the edge of the road. *Swoosh,* and *swoosh* again.

"What was that?" cried James. They stopped on the side of the road. *Swoosh* for the third time, like a dive bomber. It was a magpie swooping down on them, protecting its nest and family from these cyclist intruders.

"Just as well, we are wearing helmets," said Aroha. "Although they wouldn't actually hit you, just want to scare you off." *Swoosh* again. "Come on, James, we had better get going and leave this territorial protector." One more *swoosh* and they got away unscathed but it was a little frightening, nevertheless.

Eventually, they came to an off-road rest area. "Let's stop here for a bite to eat and drink," said James.

"OK," replied Aroha. They sat on the wooden bench eating their dry bread and a sip of water to help swallow and digest the gluggy bread.

"Why didn't you take some cakes?" asked Aroha.

"I had to quickly find something," James replied, "before cook would see me and all I could see was bread."

They watched the traffic as it passed at such speed, trucks and cars, caravans and campervans. "I wonder where the campervans are going," said James.

"Probably on an adventure just like us."

The roads were getting longer. James was getting tired of the same scenery for ages and ages, then he started, *"One thousand green bottles hanging on the wall, one thousand green bottles hanging on the wall and if one green bottle should accidentally fall, there'll be nine hundred and ninety-nine green bottles hanging on the wall. Nine hundred and ninety-nine green bottles hanging on the wall, nine hundred and ninety-nine green bottles hanging on the wall..."*

It was lunch time and they parked up and had their lunch by the side of the road. "I don't like it here," said Aroha, "we are too close to the traffic. Let's just climb over the fence out of harm's way."

"What's for lunch?" asked James. "Well, jolly good old-fashioned bread." *Thump, thump.*

"What was that?" said James.

"I'm not sure," replied Aroha.

They looked around across the paddock; nothing to be seen. *Thump, thump* and a *bellow*, a cloud of dust in the distance. "Still can't see much," said James. Then suddenly, "It's—it's—it's a bull! Quick, back over the fence."

They just made it and the bull was right there, snorting and bellowing as he was kicking up the dust.

"*Phew*, that was close!" said Aroha.

"Yes, and I left my bread there," said James, "and I am not going back to get it."

There were a few morsels of bread left in the backpack, which they ate quite hurriedly. Another half hour rest after lunch and then off again on their journey. The light breeze continued blowing southward, helping them on their journey.

On and on they rode, it was now three p.m. and they stopped for a short break.

"Not long now," said Aroha, "and we will be in Te Kao."

A drink of water and the last of the bread, starting to go a bit stale. Helmets on, they started off again. The day still mild, not too hot, made for pleasant cycling. A bit of an uphill climb made their legs ache a bit.

"*Six hundred and fifty-two green bottles hanging on the wall...*" And so, James continued his famous solo.

Chapter 2
-34.651371,172.970395

It would be another twenty minutes, and Aroha excitedly exclaimed, "I think I see it, just past the row of pines!" With all their strength, they raced the last three hundred metres and finally reached the Te Kao local store. First and most importantly, they jumped off their bikes, ran into the store, bought an ice cream each and sat on the outdoor bench.

"This is just heaven," said James. "I haven't had ice cream for years. I'm going to have ice cream every day."

There is a legend where in Te Kao, Te Houtaewa of the Te Aupōuri tribe, a strong athlete stole some kumera from the Te Rarawa tribe and ran the distance of ninety-mile beach (Te Oneroa-a-Tōhē) and subsequently out-running those that gave chase. Initiated in 2003, the legend is honoured each year by a race from the Maunganui Bluff to the Paripari Domain as a symbol of peace. A kumera is given to Te Rarawa by Te Aupōuri.

A Ratana Church is located at Te Kao. The design of the Ratana Church includes two bell towers with the words 'Arepa' and 'Omeka' (which in Greek means

Alpha and Omega — the beginning and the end) with a star and crescent moon set up on top of the towers.

Aroha and James went back into the store for a small bottle of milk to make their morning Weet-Bix a bit more juicy and more palatable to eat. Also, a small block of cheese, a packet of crackers, and an apple each for their tea. Plus, a block of chocolate. They biked a couple of hundred metres south, there was a paddock with quite a bit of scrub growing, ideal for concealing two pup tents. They had to be careful climbing over the fence with the top wire being barbed. Aroha passed the bikes over to James. They found a small clearing surrounded by tall scrub, pitched their tents and had a rest before their evening meal, Aroha glued to her book and James recounting the day's adventures for his diary.

Next morning, after a fantastic Weet-Bix and milk breakfast, they rode back to the store for a few more provisions including water and begrudgingly bought a fresh loaf of bread, although this time accompanied with a small jar of jam. Time to set off again.

The weather continued to be kind to them, a gentle northerly breeze helped them on their way. They passed through much of the same rural scenery, lots of beef cattle and heaps of sheep. They travelled about thirteen kilometres and came to Rarawa Beach Road.

"Let's go to the beach!" exclaimed James. "I think it's only about five kilometres off the State Highway."

"OK," Aroha replied, "it will be nice to get some sea air."

And twenty-five minutes later, they were at the beach riding straight onto the sand. The sand there is unique, it is like a fine white powder and gives the beach a beautiful appearance.

"Mmmmm, breathe in that lovely sea air," said Aroha.

They sat on the sand and decided to have their lunch. As they ate, they gazed out beyond the sea at the far distant horizon. The sand was warm from the brilliant sunny day but it was still a little too cold for a swim. After a rest and a short walk along the beach, they were back on their bikes heading towards the turn-off onto the highway. They travelled past a marae and the Ngataki School and passed the Henderson Bay Road turn-off which is another access to the beach.

"Only about nine kilometres to Houhora and we can rest up for the day," said Aroha.

"Three hundred and ninety-eight green bottles hanging on the wall—"

"Please stop that ridiculous song," demanded Aroha, but James wouldn't hear of it and on and on he went.

Eventually, they arrived in Houhora. In the distance, they saw the imposing site of Houhora Mountain. When the Pacific navigator Kupe arrived in New Zealand, he thought the mountain was a whale which he named Tohoraha (whale). When James Cook discovered New Zealand in 1769, he named the large hill Mount Camel because of its shape. Both names are used to refer to the mount.

"Let's go to Pukenui," said James. "It's only another three kilometres."

"Good idea," said Aroha. Just out of Pukenui, they saw a plantation of manuka with some clear patches in the paddock.

"This looks like a good place," said Aroha. "At least the manuka will shelter us from the highway. I'll just have a look for somewhere to set up." She climbed over the fence while James took guard over the bikes and backpacks on the side of the road.

"*Aaaaaaaaaaaaaaaaaaaaaaaaaaaaaaaaaaaahhhhh hhhhhhhhhhhhhhhhhhhhhh!*" screamed Aroha. She came running back and scrambled over the fence. "Quick, go, quick, go! Bees!"

Yes, there were hundreds of them defending their hives from the intruder. Off they biked as fast as they could for two kilometres.

"I must stop," said Aroha, totally out of breath. "They stung me!" she exclaimed. There were two stings on her right arm. Aroha poured a little water on the stings to cool the affected area.

They rode on a little further. "Look," said James, "an ice cream shop with real berries ice cream. Can we afford it?" asked James.

"Well, they might be a bit expensive but we might just have enough," replied Aroha.

"So many different flavours, let's have strawberry, with blue berries. *Yum*, they are delicious!"

They sat in the twilight sun consuming the luscious ice cream in two minutes, then BRAIN FREEZE.

"That hurts." They held their heads trying to warm up. Slowly, the headaches passed away, and they were back to normal.

"Next time, we will eat ice cream a lot slower!" suggested Aroha.

Out of sight of traffic, they eventually found a place off the road to pitch their tents. Settling in for the night, they pored over the map and decided to head off to Waipapakauri. It's about thirty kilometres but they decided on that destination and would stop about halfway for lunch and a break in Waiharara.

It was a cooler morning shrouded with high cloud. "I wonder if it will rain?" James asked. "I don't fancy biking in the pouring rain."

"I think it should be OK," said Aroha. "We should be able to get to Waipapakauri before any rain sets in."

They took off at a slower pace. A southerly head wind was picking up, making the journey a little harder. They eventually arrived at Waiharara. There was not too much to see so they carried on a little further until they came to a turn-off directing to 'Gumdiggers Buried Forest 3km'.

"Let's take a look," said Aroha, "it's not very far."

"OK," muttered James who didn't want to get off the beaten track, especially with the weather closing in. They came to Gumdiggers Park.

Gumdiggers Park is a Kauri gum-digging site over a hundred years old. Māori and European settlers began gum digging in 1860s which evolved into a lucrative industry, with some trees being over one hundred thousand years old. Presentations at the park describe the events which may have caused the forest destruction. Aroha was intrigued by this fascinating historic event; whilst they wanted to go into the park, they felt they could not afford the entry fees of $6 each as they barely had enough for food.

They learnt from the friendly staff that Kauri Gum is in fact fossilised resin from sap of the Kauri tree. The sap leaks out through fractures or cracks in the bark and injury sites of the tree. When exposed to the air, the sap hardens to a type of copal. Over time, kauri gum will eventually harden and takes the form of amber.

The largest living Kauri tree in New Zealand is known as Tāne Mahuta (God of the forest) and grows in the Waipoua Forest sanctuary. It is estimated at twelve hundred years, the circumference around the trunk is fourteen metres and has a height of fifty-one metres. Kauri are known to live to two thousand years old, and records show as much as four thousand years old.

After a wander around, they set off again to Waipapakauri. The weather was becoming bleaker, clouds gathering and getting darker.

"I think I can feel some spots of rain," said Aroha. "We will need to bike faster," although the head wind did not help. They passed West Coast Road, which is a turn-off to ninety-mile beach. As much as they would have liked to spend some time at the beach, their better judgement made for faster pedalling to Waipapakauri.

The wind was now really starting to pick up. They biked on and over the Waipapakauri Bridge, where just to the left past the bridge was a dense area of trees. "Let's go in there and pitch our tents," said James.

The spits of rain were getting more frequent. With no time to lose, they set up camp and just managed to climb inside their tents seconds before the deluge arrived. It poured and it poured. James called out to Aroha, "I would call this fat rain," as the rain drops were large and heavy.

Aroha called back, "I think it's best we stay in our tents for the rest of the day and night. Going out in this weather, we would get soaked." James agreed and they both settled down with a book before bed.

Waipapakauri accommodated a small aerodrome in 1933. At the outbreak of World War II, the aerodrome was taken over by the Royal New Zealand Air Force and used as a base. During the war, the base was enlarged several times to cope with air traffic of bombers and fighter planes. Upgrades to the airbase included the installation of fortified permanent structures.

There are now only some building remnants as the airbase was closed shortly after the war. However, what was the hospital has been converted to the Waipapakauri Hotel, still in operation today.

Chapter 3
-35.116206,173.267637

Next morning, James peeked out of his tent, the sun was shining. No one would have even guessed that it rained during the night.

"Aroha, Aroha, wakey, wakey," called James.

"What time is it?" asked Aroha, sleepily rubbing her eyes.

"Time for breakfast," James replied. "Look how sunny it is," he continued.

Aroha couldn't believe her eyes; she had had visions of staying in her tent for the next few days sheltering from the fat rain.

After breakfast, they waited around for a bit, allowing the sun to dry the tents off before packing them up.

"Well, it's off to Kaitaia," said Aroha. "Only thirteen kilometres, we should arrive well before lunch time." They eventually set off, passing through Awanui, situated by the Awanui River where it flows into Rangaunu Bay. Awanui used to be a river port but has ceased operating. A recreational port has been established at Unahi which is approximately three kilometres north of the Awanui township.

Finally, they arrived in Kaitaia. They knew it was Kaitaia as the welcome sign said, *Haere Mai, Dobrodošli*, Welcome To, all meaning welcome to in Māori, Dalmation, and English representative of Māori, Dalmatian, and European heritage. The name Kaitaia means ample food, kai being the Māori word for food. With a population of about five thousand, it was by far the largest town Aroha and James had visited. They parked their bikes and with their backpacks in tow, they wandered around the township.

After some exploration, they were back on their bikes. Only a few minutes' ride and they were in the country again with trees providing the perfect shelter and out of sight of the main road, right beside the Awanui River. They made camp and called for a conference to work out what to do next.

"Well," said Aroha, "we have no money, very little left to eat and exhausted from the travel. What do we do?"

"I know exactly," said James, "let's go fruit picking. There must be some berry farms close by and maybe if we stay for say two weeks, we should earn enough to continue our adventure."

"Now that's a smart idea," said Aroha, "why didn't I think of that! We'll finish unpacking and then ride back into town and get a newspaper to see what jobs are going."

They were soon on their way again; unfortunately, though, they didn't have enough for a newspaper. They sat on a bench at the Remembrance Park next to a man reading a newspaper, with a dog sitting obediently next to him.

"I wonder if he would give it to us when he has finished with it," whispered James.

After scrutinising each word on the back page, the man said to them, "Well there's not much news in here today, only filled with ads for jobs."

Aroha and James looked at each other, then James boldly asked the man, "Can we have the paper if you are finished with it?"

He offered it to them. "Come on, Bradley," he called to the dog, and off they went.

They came to the job vacancies section, and there they saw an advertisement for pickers at a strawberry farm only two kilometres from town. Jumping on their bikes, they were off. It wasn't long before they reached the farm, they went to a building which sort of looked like an office and packing shed.

"What can I do for you?" came a gruff voice. With his head poking out of the office window, a long beard and frizzy hair, he looked like the nutty professor.

"We saw your ad in the newspaper and would like to get a job picking strawberries."

"Shouldn't you two be at school, you aren't running away from the police, are you?"

Aroha thought quickly and said, "Oh no, we are not in any trouble. We are on work experience and would like to work on a berry farm for two weeks. We want to experience all types of farming."

"Well, don't hang around outside," said the man. "Come in, come on in.

"My name is Hector and I own this berry farm. I have thirty pickers and I need another twenty. I expect a proper full day's work and I don't want any slacking."

"We will give it our best," said Aroha.

"OK," replied Hector. "Seven a.m., start tomorrow morning."

They were up at six a.m. the next morning, had a quick breakfast and the three km ride to the farm. Reporting at the office, Hector detailed off all the pickers to their respective areas. Each was handed a small wooden trolley with wheels. In the trolley were two cardboard cartons and packs of plastic punnets. Each picker was allotted a number, 10 and 11 respectively for Aroha and James. Advay, one of the team leaders on a work permit from India, showed them how to pick the fruit. "Pack them into the plastic punnets and when the carton is full, lift it off the trolley for someone to pick it up and replace with an empty carton."

It was heavy work and all were pleased when they were allowed a break at morning tea.

Biscuits were provided with tea or coffee. James had not four but five biscuits (they were only allowed one or two). Only a fifteen-minute break and then back into it. James could not resist the temptation; one strawberry whole into his mouth. *That was so sweet, I'll just have one or two more,* he thought. He carried on picking and packing and eating.

"Don't eat so many," said Aroha, "it will make you feel sick."

Advay joined the conversation and also warned James not to eat too many. "I'm OK," said James. "I know what I am doing."

More berries picked, more berries eaten, James was getting slower and slower.

"It's lunch time, a longer break so make the most of it," said Advay.

Aroha looked behind her, and in a distance, she saw James struggling. As he got closer, she noticed strawberry flesh all over James' mouth and face.

"I can't look at another strawberry, I feel sick," said James.

"What did we tell you, but you wouldn't listen."

Despite packing his own lunch, James didn't have anything to eat.

"I feel so full." he groaned.

Aroha suggested he take a nap seeing they had half an hour break. It didn't take three minutes and James was fast asleep.

"Back to work," Advay called.

"That was an extremely fast half hour," said James, feeling slightly better. "I am never going to eat another strawberry," he muttered as they walked back to their trolleys.

The work day finally came to a close, Advay told them all to pack up and take their trolleys to the packing shed. Back on their bikes, they rode off to the camp. After a bite to eat and a short read and diary entry, they both agreed on an early night, stumbled into their sleeping bags, but after a few more "I'm so full" groans from James, they fell asleep.

Another fine morning greeted them. Not a moment to lose, breakfast, teeth and ready for the road back to berry picking. All day long, they worked, and you'll never guess, James didn't eat a single strawberry. James was just about to unload another carton when he felt something behind him. Turning around, there was a collie sheep dog sitting, wagging its tail and gazing at James. James crouched down, stroking his new-found friend.

Aroha came over and said, "What a lovely dog, he must belong to the farm."

James called out to Advay, "Is this the owner's dog?"

"No," said Advay. "I have never seen him before, might be a stray."

"I'm going to call him Timmy from *The Famous Five*," said James. He picked up the dog's front paw and gently shook it, introducing himself as James and naming the dog Timmy.

"Time to pack up," Advay announced.

They all headed for the packing shed, dropped off the work gear and went to their bikes.

"No, Timmy," said James, "you have to stay here. I'll be back tomorrow, will see you then."

After another stroke, James and Aroha set off to their camp. Lifting their bikes over the fence, they climbed over and went back to their tents. They were preparing their tea when suddenly, Aroha exclaimed, "Your friend is here!"

To James' surprise, Timmy had followed them and decided to make himself at home at the camp. James was so pleased to see this welcomed visitor. After tea, they had a game of chase in the paddock with Timmy leading the charge. Starting to get a little late, Aroha and James decided to turn in for the evening. Timmy followed James into his tent and made himself comfortable next to James' sleeping bag.

Just before six a.m., James felt a wet slobbering sensation. Opening his eyes, he saw it was Timmy licking James' face, trying to wake him up.

"All right, all right," said James, "I know, it's time to get up."

Aroha and James got themselves ready and then were off to work. As soon as they arrived at the farm, Timmy was already waiting to greet them.

"How did you get here so quickly?" asked James. After some significant patting and stroking, they went to their picking area with Timmy trotting beside them.

"Does Hector have a dog?" James asked Advay.

"He does but they don't come here with the pickers, they are guard dogs."

I wonder if Hector has some dog biscuits that I can give Timmy, James thought, *I'll ask him at lunch time.*

During the lunch break, James went in to see Hector. He told Hector the story of his new companion and asked if Hector could spare a few dog biscuits. Hector bought biscuits by the sack full and was happy to give a small bag of biscuits for Timmy. By now, Timmy could smell what James had in the bag, he pushed closer to James with his tail wagging even harder.

"OK, Timmy, you win," said James. "One now and another later on." Back to work they carried on until five p.m.

"Time to go," said Aroha.

Dropping off their tools at the packing shed, James put a few dog biscuits in his pocket and left the bag with his tools. "Later," said James to Timmy, "stop pushing."

They got back to their camp and Timmy was already waiting there for them. "How did you get here so quickly?" asked James. Timmy just wagged his tail harder.

Aroha and James remained a little over two weeks in Kaitaia. On the morning of the last day, James was frantically searching everywhere in amongst bushes and down by the river. "Timmy, Timmy, where are you? Come on, boy." But no Timmy.

Aroha said, "He has left the same way as he arrived, just appeared and then disappeared without a trace. He may have sensed that we will be on the move again," she said, trying to console James who was getting quite upset.

"I loved that dog," James said, "I thought we would be able to keep him."

Aroha replied, "It was really good that he became friends with us during our stay here, but it would not be possible to keep him as he would not be able to travel with us."

"You're right, I suppose," said James.

They cycled to the farm for one last day. Hector called them into his office.

"So, you are leaving us today," he said.

"Yes," replied Aroha, "we need to be on our way."

He handed them their wages. "You have been good kids, maybe one day you will be back for more job experience."

They thanked him and asked if they could finish up at lunchtime as they had a few things to get in town. He said that would be fine. They picked up their tools from the shed and went picking for just half of the day. At lunch, they farewelled the rest of the team and thanked Advay for his friendly help and set off into town.

They parked up their bikes, sat on a bench and counted up their earnings. "We have $218 between us," said Aroha, "that should help us get a fair way."

They went to a cut price variety store to buy a shower proof poncho each and a high vis vest, some sun block and insect repellent. Then off to the supermarket to buy non-perishable food items and toiletries. After more of a wander around town, they made off to camp.

At camp after tea, James said he was just going for a short walk. Secretly, he was searching for Timmy but didn't tell Aroha. With a deep sigh, he abandoned the search as Timmy was nowhere to be found. Aroha was looking at the map and suggested they only travel about eighteen kilometres to Raetea North Side camping ground which is just off the highway.

Chapter 4
-35.166921,173.433839

All packed and ready to go, they put on their high vis vests which they wore on every cycle trip from there on. As they rode off, they both waved out and said, "Goodbye, Kaitaia."

"I really enjoyed it here," said Aroha.

"Me too," said James, "especially when Timmy arrived."

They came across some loose gravel on the road.

"Careful," said Aroha, "some of the stones are a bit large."

James wasn't paying much attention, probably thinking about Timmy, when suddenly his wheel hit against a stone and he came crashing down. A car coming up from behind swerved, skidding in the loose stones and came to an abrupt stop. The driver jumped out of his car and came around to James, he thought he had hit James. Aroha raced back, and they helped James back on his feet. Fortunately, he wasn't hurt, just a bit of damage to his pride.

"Are you OK?" asked the driver.

"Yes, I'm OK, thanks," replied James, "just a bit shaken from the incident. The wheel must have slipped on the loose stones."

"It looks a bit dangerous to me," said the driver, "probably fell off a trailer or truck. I'll call the police; they will know who to get hold of to have it removed." Off they all went. This time, James was keeping a bit more focused on the environment around him.

They reached Raetea close to lunch time, had to turn off the highway along a short gravel access and over a stream ford into the camp site.

"What a beautiful place," said Aroha.

A clear grass area for tents and campervans surrounded by native bush and a crystal-clear stream running alongside the camp ground. There were no other campers at the time, just nature's beauty with the songs of Tui conversing with each other. The camp site is maintained by Department of Conservation (DOC) and the best thing is that it is free of charge. They set up camp, made lunch and sat by the stream watching the glistening ripples flow by.

"Let's go for a swim after lunch," said Aroha.

"Sound like fun," replied James. Lunch took all of five minutes and into the water they went. It was a warm day and the water wasn't too freezing; although, it was on the cool side. Having dried themselves, they thought they would explore the bush. Huge Kauri towered above them, forming a canopy covering shrubs and younger trees. Beneath these grow a variety of ferns and mosses.

"What's THAT?" asked James backtracking a couple of metres.

"What?" said Aroha.

"Under there," James said, pointing to a fern.

"I can't see a thing," said Aroha.

James picked up a stick and pointed right at the creature.

"Oh that, it's pretty big, isn't it!" said Aroha. "It's a Kauri snail."

Many times' larger than an ordinary garden variety of snail and what's more, it is carnivorous. Which means, it feeds on earthworms, insects, insect larvae, slugs and small snails. Aroha picked it up, it was quite large and could have measured at least sixty millimetres.

Aroha placed the snail under the fern and they strolled back to the camp site. It was late afternoon/evening drawing in, and sand flies and mosquitoes were starting to make their presence known.

"Time for some insect repellent," said James.

"Yes, quickly," said Aroha, "before I get eaten alive." They studied the map and decided the next stop to be Umawera. It is a little further than their usual daily twenty-km excursion by only approximately five kilometres. However, they did need to negotiate the Mangamuka Gorge which is quite a winding hilly stretch of road. After tea and some reading, they called it a day fairly early to be rejuvenated for the next day's adventure.

It was quite overcast early morning with just a few spits of rain. They set off as soon as possible, also donned in their shower-proof ponchos just in case the rain got heavier. Getting closer to the gorge, the road gradually began to wind. The scenery was stunning, with native lush bush painting a natural masterpiece, attempting to hide the bland tar road. Some of the road was a little tricky to negotiate as there was very little room between the white line on the side of the road and the road edge which slipped away into the water table. Vehicles were also passing quite close to the cyclists where the road narrowed. They stopped at a wide gravel area off the road for a breather and just to take in the beautiful scenery. Back on their bikes, they rode on to Mangamuka where they had a longer break and lunch. The Mangamuka Forest is home to many giant kauri trees. In 1952, the Omahuta Kauri Sanctuary was set up to protect the trees and allow the public access to the giants of the forest.

Next, toward Umawera, only ten kilometres further, to the small community area.

"Gruntled… Gruntled, I am gruntled."

"What are you talking about?" asked Aroha.

"I am gruntled," said James yet again. "I don't know what it means but my friend Jon at the orphanage kept saying he was gruntled, only in the next sentence saying he was disgruntled."

"Well," said Aroha, "gruntled means pleased, satisfied, contented; whilst disgruntled means angry or dissatisfied."

"So, you mean," asked James, "that you can have the two words in one sentence; something like, I am gruntled because it is fine weather and at the same time disgruntled that I have to bike up this steep hill."

"I suppose you can," said Aroha.

"Well," said James, "I am gruntled that my bike is so shiny, but I am very disgruntled that I haven't eaten for two hours. I am gruntled because… I am disgruntled because… Gruntled/disgruntled, gruntled/disgruntled,"

"Don't you ever give up?" asked Aroha.

"No," said James. "Gruntled/disgruntled…" Eventually, he stopped and all was peaceful again for a short while.

They reached Umawera and camped up. Aroha suggested that they get an early night as she would like to veer off State Highway 1 to go to Waitangi which is about fifty-seven kilometres.

"What do you want to go there for?" asked James.

"Just interested about the history of Māori/Pākehā," said Aroha.

Next day, they had Waitangi in their sights. James was a little annoyed that they had to bike further and off the State Highway but he tried not to show it as Aroha was quite interested in its history. Again, the weather was pleasant and a very light tail breeze helped them on their way. Waitangi is a locality in the Bay of Islands.

The name Waitangi means weeping waters. It is the location where the Treaty of Waitangi was signed on 6 February 1840 on the grounds of the residence of James Busby (Resident Minister of the British government).

Initially, some forty Māori chiefs led by Hone Heke signed the Māori version of the Treaty on 6 February 1840. By September of the same year, a further five hundred chiefs signed copies of the document. British sovereignty was proclaimed on 21 May 1840. A national holiday is celebrated each year on 6 February as a remembrance of the treaty signing.

After the treaty was signed, Okiato in the Bay of Islands was determined as the capital city. In 1841, New Zealand separated from New South Wales (Australia) and was made a colony in its own right with the capital being moved to Auckland. Some twenty-four years later, the capital was again moved this time to Wellington.

BANG! That was James' back tyre. It gave him such a fright that he nearly fell off his bike. They stopped on the side of the road and peered at the wheel to assess the damage. "Doesn't look very good," said James. "I must have ridden over a nail or something. What do you think we should do in the middle of nowhere?" he asked.

Aroha said, "Well, maybe there might be a kind person who can give us a lift to a bike repair shop."

They tried waving cars and trucks and buses down, but no one would stop, they were all travelling quite fast. Eventually, a man in an old ute pulled up.

"What seems to be the trouble?" he asked.

"My bike tyre has a puncture," said James, "and we're looking for a bike repair shop."

"You won't find anything around here," he said. "Your best bet would be a petrol station; they might have a car repair shop and probably be able to fix your bike. Where are you headed?" he asked.

"We are going to Waitangi," Aroha replied.

"Well, that's where I am going. You can throw the bikes up on the tray and you will need to sit on the tray as well as I haven't any room in the cab."

They were so pleased, they hurriedly put the bikes on the back and clambered onto the ute tray.

The man said, "Sit back and hold on, I won't go too fast." He drove fairly slowly as the ute rattled and groaned and they wondered if it would last out the distance to Waitangi.

Eventually arriving at Waitangi, he dropped them off at a petrol station and pointed out the direction they should take and that they would come to a sign indicating 'Waitangi Treaty Grounds'.

They went to the petrol station and enquired if someone could fix the puncture. One of the mechanics, Dave, came over, had a look at the wheel and said, "Yep, I can probably fix it. You'll need to leave it with me for about an hour."

Aroha and James decided to have lunch whilst the bike was getting fixed. "It's the quickest fifty kilometres we have gone," said James. "I wish we can have a motor on our bikes to make cycling quicker and easier."

"No such luxury," said Aroha. They found a spot to have their lunch.

They strolled back to the petrol station and sure enough, the bike was repaired. "How much do we owe you?" asked Aroha.

"Let's make it $15," replied Dave.

Aroha handed over the money and they rode off to the treaty grounds.

They biked along the beach front. "What beautiful scenery," said Aroha, and James agreed. They came to a fairly long one-way bridge which fortunately had a separate pedestrian and cycling lane. Past the bridge, they eventually arrived at the visitor centre and Treaty House. They made enquiries about seeing the events but despite children under the age of eighteen years had free access, they had to be accompanied by parent or caregiver. So unfortunately, weren't able to attend any events; however, they did pick up a brochure and wandered around some of the grounds. Saddling up again, they biked a little further around the grounds and came to the Hobson Memorial. The plaque on this stone structure is in memory of William Hobson, governor of New Zealand (1840–1842).

The grounds cover a fairly large area which accommodates a museum, ceremonial war canoe (waka), a flagstaff situated on the site where the Treaty of Waitangi was signed. The three official flags are — Te Kara, the flag of The United Tribes of New Zealand (the earliest), the Union flag (from 1840) and the New Zealand flag (from 1902). The Treaty House at Waitangi was the residence of James Busby. A beautifully carved meeting house Te Whare Rūnanga (the House of Assembly) which faces the Treaty House was opened on 6 February 1940.

"Oi, do you want to join in?" came a voice from behind some shrubs. "We are two players short for a game of soccer."

James was there like a shot. Aroha came over too. Whilst the game was totally disorganised, all had a lot of fun UNTIL when James was standing in the middle of the imaginary-lined soccer confines looking at a black bird in a tree, the soccer ball hit smack on the left side of his head, powered by the biggest, roundest, strongest ten-year-old you ever did see. James hit the deck flat on his back. All eleven of them gathered around, and Aroha attempted to pull him up.

James opened his eyes. "I can see lots of stars," he said.

They managed to sit him up, calling time out. They all had a bit of a break while James got himself back together again. Staggering up, he and Aroha went for a short wander around the grounds, then said goodbye to their team mates and biked to a secluded bush area where they could pitch their tents.

Chapter 5
-35.379685,174.064684

Next morning, rather than cycling back to Highway 1, they decided to travel south on Highway 11 to Kawakawa which meets up with Highway 1. It was a fairly slow ride with a southerly head wind slowing their pace. Only eighteen kilometres, it didn't take long to reach their destination, they made it just before lunch. "What an unusual town," James uttered. Colourful sculptures, mosaics, copper and cobblestones formed the design of the town's public toilets, like nothing you've ever seen before. The architect Austrian-born Friedensreich Hundertwasser who lived in Kawakawa gifted these ornately sculptured toilets to the town.

Kawakawa is also known for the railway track that runs through the centre of town. The track was established during gold mining in the area, still operating today by the Bay of Islands' Vintage Railway.

After a short lunch, a decision was made to carry on to Waiomio, only five kilometres further. Aroha pointed out the unusual landscape of huge limestone formations. Inside the caves, you will find the famous New Zealand glow-worm. The glow-worm is in fact a fly as compared to the glow-worm in Europe, a beetle.

The life cycle of the glow-worm starts as an egg, it hatches in the form of a larvae and then into a pupa in a cocoon. After about two weeks, the fly emerges from the cocoon. Except for the egg, the glow-worm emits a blueish green glow in its larvae, pupa, and fly stages of life. The glow is brightest in its larvae form.

On arrival, the scenery was so beautiful and tranquil that they decided to go for a short bush walk. Some of the limestone formations appear as pillars, enormous boulders and huge solid slabs. Some of the shapes even took the form of furniture. After more exploration, Aroha and James cycled to a small clearing surrounded by bush, a good spot to camp for the night.

Next day, after some deliberation, they agreed to stay another night to make themselves cycling-fit for the long leg of the journey to Whangarei, some fifty kilometres. Whilst around twenty kilometres was their comfortable stretch, they were eager to get to the city as they were in need of extra cash and thought it easier to get some work in a larger town. As it happened, the next day was raining, so the order of the day — relax, eat, read and maybe go for a walk if the rain eased.

The following day was still overcast but not raining.

"At least it won't be hot for travelling," said James.

On careful study of their maps, they decided they would stop for lunch at Hikurangi some thirty-four kilometres. They would pass through Maromaku,

Towai, and Hūkerenui, and then a further seventeen kilometres to Whangarei.

They were getting close to Hikurangi and decided to turn off onto King Street to have a look at the Waro Scenic Reserve. Administered by the Conservation department, the track through this 7.5-hectare reserve takes you through open grassland around spectacular limestone formations. The track follows the route of a historic horse tramline, built in about 1900.

"I'm the king of the castle," shouted James, standing on a high limestone ledge which he managed to scramble up before Aroha had even reached its base.

"You be careful up there," called Aroha, "we don't want another accident."

As she was looking up at James and the surrounding landscape, Aroha didn't notice the sink hole she was just about to fall into. "*Aaaaaaaaaaahhh!*"

James heard the cry but couldn't see anyone. He came down from the towering limestone. "Where are you?" he called.

"Down here," came the reply. Fortunately, a shallow sink hole, nevertheless deep enough for a small child to fall into and not be seen. "'We don't want another accident,' famous last words."

"All right, all right," said Aroha, dusting herself down.

"What a superb play area," said James, "high limestone towers, sink holes, caves and lots of trees and foliage. I can just imagine having war games here with my friends."

They walked along the track a little further and soon turned back to get to Hikurangi by lunch time.

It was only a short bike ride to the Hikurangi township where it was time for a rest, lunch and, of course, an ice cream. After a bit of a wander, they set off down George Street connecting to the highway, passing through Kamo, a small township within the Whangarei district.

Kamo developed as a coal mining town in the 1870s. After some eighty years, the mines were depleted of coal and closed in 1955. In the late nineteenth century, hot spring spa baths were opened to the public. The hot springs were considered beneficial to health due to their mineral content.

"Are we there yet?" called James.

"Not too far," Aroha replied.

"My legs are sore, my back hurts, I'm getting a headache, my bum is sore, my hands have cramp, my neck is stiff!" exclaimed James.

"Is there anything else wrong?" asked Aroha. "What about your hair, is your hair sore?"

"It's been a long ride," protested James, "and I am so tired."

"Not too far now," said Aroha in a reassuring tone, "we'll be there before you know it."

Whangarei is a city in the Northland region. The Māori iwi Ngāpuhi (the largest iwi in New Zealand) occupied Whangarei from the early nineteenth century.

Marsden Point at the southern end of Whangarei harbour is home to New Zealand's only oil refinery which opened in 1964 on Bream Bay. Northland Port was also established at Marsden Point in 2002, primarily for the export of timber. To the north east is Mount Parihaka and the Parihaka Scenic Reserve. A walk in the reserve brings you to the 26-metre-high Whangarei Falls on the Hātea River. A track continues to the base of the climb up the 241-metre-high mount. Dobbies Track winds along the sometimes-steep sections of the mount with dense bush on either side of the track. The mount is a volcanic dome and is about twenty million years old. There is a war memorial at the top and a viewing platform which provides for a panoramic view of the city.

Thirty minutes had passed and there it was, the city of Whangarei. Both exhausted from their long trip, they sat on a park bench and hoed into several energy bars.

"What now?" asked James.

Aroha suggested they go for a walk around the town and see what was offering for paid work.

"How about this place?" said James, already wandering into a café. Aroha asked the café assistant if there were any job vacancies, the answer was no. They went to another and another. Eight more cafés and no luck.

"We'll never get any work," said James in a very sober tone.

"Don't worry," said Aroha, "we'll find something."

They decided to call it a day and biked out a little distance to pitch their tents in a small, wooded area off the main road. Digging deep into their backpacks, they managed to scrape up just enough food for their tea, with a little left over for breakfast.

"We'll have to get a job soon," said James, "or I'll die of starvation."

Next day after breakfast, they set off again back into the main centre.

"Look," said Aroha, "the circus is coming to town. Let's go and watch them setting up."

The circus was being held at the William Fraser Memorial Park. They wandered around by the tents, there was so much activity going on they had to be careful not to get in anyone's way.

"What do you think about working at the circus?" said James.

"Not sure about that," replied Aroha, "what would we actually do?"

James asked one of the workers who should they see about a job.

"The Ring mistress," the worker replied, "Miss Prudence McKenzie, you call her Miss Pru. She is over in the white and blue caravan. You can't miss it; it has butterflies painted all over it."

On finding the caravan tucked between some large tents, Aroha knocked on the door.

"Yes? What do you want," a lady in a black jacket with matching but sparkling waistcoat, black flared trousers and black patent leather shoes opened the door and towered over the children, as she was a little over six feet tall.

"We wondered if you might have a job for us?" asked Aroha.

"No, sorry," said Miss Pru, "all jobs taken, I'm afraid."

"OK, thanks," said Aroha and they both walked away very disappointed.

By one of the tents there were five poodles tied on leashes. "Aren't they lovely!" said Aroha.

Kneeling down beside them, she stroked them and they started playing and licking her face. Miss Pru came over and said, "You are very good with them, they certainly like you. They often bark at other people. Maybe I can give you a job, looking after them, taking them for walks, feeding them, and making sure they are always clean."

"That's fantastic," said Aroha, "when can I start?"

"Right now," said Miss Pru. Just at that moment, Fred came over, his arms raised in the air.

"How can I do my work when all my assistants leave me?" said Fred in a panic.

"What's wrong now?" Miss Pru demanded. "My assistant has quit and now I have no one to help me with my acts."

"What about him?" Miss Pru pointed at James.

Fred looked James over. "Can you run, dance, make faces, fall over, do roly polys, carry buckets, blow up balloons?"

"Yes, I can do all of that," said James confidently.

"Then follow me," said Fred.

Daisy Fellows trained the poodles for various circus acts, she showed Aroha what to do and be a companion for them. So, the first task was to take them for a walk, all five of them, at the same time. They crisscrossed and trotted in different directions, the leashes became tangled and Aroha got her foot caught in a tent guide rope. Down she went, the dogs scattered and Daisy was getting stomach cramps from laughing so much.

"That's not how you do it," said Daisy. "There is an easier way. Meg, Joe and Flo walk on the right side and they are always together. Fifi and Pierre on the left." Aroha tried again with the correct combination; it worked a treat.

Aroha was grooming the dogs.

"Well? What d'ye think?"

Aroha turned around, and there he was. Jacket, trousers and shoes way oversized, bowler hat with yellow hair attached, red nose, painted face — yes, James was a circus clown.

"You look great!" said Aroha. "I didn't recognise you."

"I am featuring with Fred," James said. "Also, Fred mentioned that we can set up our tents behind those larger ones so that they will be out of the way, and that we can stay here for the next two weeks, the duration of the whole performance."

They finished for the day at five p.m. Biked over to where they had originally pitched their tents, took them down and went back to the park. "What's for tea?" asked James.

"Not sure at this stage," replied Aroha. "Maybe after we have set up our tents, we can go to the supermarket and get a few bits for tea."

They had just finished setting up and Fred walked past. "Are you hungry, kids? The guys are cooking up a barbeque so get in there and eat."

James couldn't believe his ears, then he couldn't believe his eyes on the huge spread that had been prepared.

"We usually have a barbeque at the end of the day whilst we are setting up. During the shows, though, we need to get our own and eat when we have time."

Aroha and James stayed for the two-week show, it took another two days to help disassemble all the tents and the big top and equipment. They were on the move again (the circus, that is), heading down to Warkworth. Aroha and James managed to secure their bikes on one of the trucks and accompanied Fred on the way. It took about two hours to arrive at the Rodney Showgrounds just north of the Warkworth township.

Warkworth holds an annual Kowhai Festival during October each year. The week-long festival has been running since 1970. Named after the Kowhai tree, the Warkworth district is known as the Kowhai Coast. Just a few kilometres south is the country's main satellite communication ground station which was constructed in 1971.

For the next two days, Aroha and James worked on setting up tents, looking after the five show dogs, and general help. It was now time to say goodbye. James thanked Fred for all his help and the opportunity to be the clown's assistant.

"When I grow up," said James, "I'm going to be a circus clown just like you, Fred."

On their bikes once again, they headed for Orewa. Orewa is a suburb of Auckland on the Hibiscus Coast. Orewa has a beach that spreads for some three kilometres. The Orewa Lions club organise the Big Dig event each year which started in the 1980s. Some one thousand sticks are buried in the beach sand. There are two roped-off sections separating the under five-year-old children from the older ones. The idea is for the children to find the sticks with small prizes given for each stick found and an entry in a bigger prize draw. All proceeds go to various charities.

"What an awesome beach!" exclaimed James, jumping off his bike as he rode onto the sand. The bike still careered several metres before it plunged into the sand. "You can see for miles," he said.

Only a few people on the beach at that time of day. They decided to have lunch on the beach and walk along the water's edge. "*Ha, ha ha, ha.*"

Aroha turned around there was James closing up on her, holding a large crab ready to place on her neck. Aroha gave such a shriek that a couple of people started to walk towards her to see what the problem was. When they saw what was going on, they just smiled with amusement and walked off. Aroha was not impressed at all.

"Throw it back into the sea," she demanded.

Reluctantly, James carefully placed it back into the water.

"Don't ever do that again!" Aroha bellowed, while James just laughed.

They biked off to a nearby reserve where they put up tents in a secluded area away from public view. It was decided an early night as their next trip was a little over thirty kilometres to Glenfield.

An early start next morning saw them travel through Silverdale which is located by the Weiti River. The name Silverdale was derived from the large number of poplar trees displaying their silver-white colour on the underside of the leaves. The trip in the main took them through rural areas, lush foliage on either side of the road; however, with an abrupt end. Entering Northcross, greater Auckland begins.

"What a lot of houses!" James exclaimed.

"Yes," said Aroha, "I suspect there will be far more as we get closer to the city."

They detoured onto Browns Bay and followed the sea shore past Rothesay, Murrays, and Mairangi bays. The views were magnificent, yellow soft sand and blue waters. They decided to have a short break by the sea shore. Browns Bay is an Auckland suburb and with Rothesay, Murrays, Mairangi, Campbell, and Castor bays form the East Coast Bays area.

"Well, we won't be able to pitch our tent here in the middle of the street or someone's garden," said James, "where are we going to sleep?"

"Just as well we earned money at the circus," said Aroha. "I think we will look for a cheap B&B."

There seemed to be quite a few B&Bs to choose from; they eventually decided on a small cottage down a narrow side street. An elderly lady invited them in. It was a bit dark inside, probably due to the small windows and dark-patterned wall paper. She charged them $40 for the night which included a cooked breakfast.

That's pretty cheap, Aroha thought to herself.

"My name is Mrs Baker," said the house owner, "and you can refer to me as Mrs Baker."

A bit odd, thought Aroha and James as they looked at each other.

Mrs Baker lived on her own and supplemented her pension by taking in lodgers.

"There is only one bedroom," she said, "with two single beds."

She left them to unpack their backpacks.

"I think she's a bit strange," whispered James.

"I think you are right," Aroha replied, "we'll just be here for one night and make an early start in the morning."

Next morning, they were treated to bacon, eggs, baked beans and toast. "Wow," said James with a mouthful of beans, "this is heaven!"

"Slow down," said Aroha, "and mind your manners."

They helped Mrs Baker clean up, handed over $40 and set off on the next leg of their journey to Manukau.

Chapter 6
-36.993719,174.883668

After a short six-kilometre bike ride, they arrived at Northcote Point where they caught a ferry to Auckland city. What a sight from the ferry, the huge Auckland metropolis coming towards them from the south.

"I've never seen such a large city," said James, "buildings everywhere reaching to the sky."

Aroha agreed but was a little anxious how they would cope in what looked like an overwhelming blanket of buildings.

Auckland (*Tāmaki Makaurau*) is the largest and most populous region in New Zealand. The region has a population of over one and a half million. The Māori name refers to 'desired by many' due to the fertile soils and natural resources. A feature of Auckland are the two harbours on either side of the city. The western harbour lies in the Tasman Sea whereas the eastern in the Pacific Ocean.

As a commemoration to the arrival of Lieutenant-Governor William Hobson, an official Anniversary Day was proclaimed for 29 January 1841. As part of the celebration, a boating regatta was held. This has become so popular that from thereon, it has been run each year.

Auckland sits on a basaltic volcanic field. A number of volcanic cones are spread across Auckland resulting in the undulating landscape of the area. The volcanic cones are now dormant but the magma beneath is still active.

Disembarking at the quay, they biked off onto St Georges Bay Road, along Parnell, Remuera, and Omahu roads and eventually onto Great South Road. This was an alternate route as cyclists cannot use motorways or the harbour bridge.

"Just keep close behind me," said Aroha, "and absolutely obey traffic rules."

"I will, I will," said James. Both were somewhat nervous immersed in the congested traffic. They arrived at Clist Crescent, the home address of the famous Rainbow's End theme park. Aroha purchased two tickets at Kidz Kingdom (that's all they could afford), hoping they wouldn't be questioned as Kidz Kingdom is for youngsters up to eight years of age. They did manage to get through, headed straight to the café for a sandwich, drink and a rest.

Next stop, some of the rides. Whilst the older kids and adults' rides looked very inviting, they were content to stick with the littlies and parents. Rather than leave it too late in the day, the pair decided to look for some accommodation for the night. They soon found a fairly cheap backpackers' venue close by.

Next day, on the road again on the Great South Road. The idea was to leave Auckland city as soon as possible to hopefully get onto some quieter roads, although that wouldn't happen for quite a few kilometres. As they rode further, buildings slowly gave way to open green paddocks and livestock grazing. It was getting close to lunchtime, with the Great South Road terminating at Bombay. They decided to buy lunch at a café within the settlement. Bombay Hills are the result of volcanic activity in the area. The landscape forms a boundary between Auckland and the Waikato region. The name Bombay refers to the name of a ship that brought settlers to the district.

They set off a short distance and found a wooded area that looked ideal for camping for the night. It was decided an early night as the next trip to Rangiriri is about forty-seven kilometres, double their typical daily jaunt.

Should they turn left, State highway 2 will eventually join with highway 1 just past Lower Hutt and will lead them to Wellington.

They left quite early to get a good start before the heat of the day set in.

"I've never seen so many in all my life." Amazed at the herd of alpacas, James said, "So many I can't even count them.".

A farmer was fixing up a fence nearby. "They look nice, don't they?" she said.

"They are beautiful!" Aroha replied. "How many do you have?"

The farmer said, "We have a hundred and fifty here and thirty-five on the lower terrace." Fiona (the farmer) continued, "There are about twenty-six thousand alpacas in New Zealand. There are some largish herds; however, most have ten or less."

"How do you cut the wool off?" asked James.

"We shear them just like shearing sheep, the difference is they are bigger. The wool is much softer and finer than sheep wool."

"Thank you for that," said Aroha, "we had better be on our way before it gets too hot."

"Bike safely," said Fiona, and off they went.

The trip was some twelve kilometres further by bike than car as they had to skirt around the Waikato Expressway. They passed through Mercer and then onto Meremere.

The history of Meremere is known for its coal fired power station during the period 1958–1991. Meremere also has a permanent drag racing facility which opened in 1973. Not far from the town is the famous Hampton Downs motorsport park that not only has a 3.8-kilometre racing circuit but also a corporate karting circuit.

"I'd love to have a go on the Go-kart circuit," said James.

"Me too," replied Aroha, "but unfortunately, we cannot afford it. We will need to find some employment soon before our funds run out."

Next stop was Rangiriri. As soon as they got there, they got off their bikes and had a lie down in a paddock. They were absolutely zonked from the long ride. Not much to see in Rangiriri itself as the main populated town area was Te Kauwhata. Whilst only some four kilometres away, they decided to stay in Rangiriri and prepare for their next journey to Huntly.

A major battle took place at Rangiriri 20–21 November 1863. It was part of what is known as the invasion of the Waikato. Heavy losses occurred on both sides, the Māori surrendered on 21 November.

Next morning was the more welcomed shorter ride to Huntly (fifteen kilometres). Originally named Rāhui Pōkeka, the town was renamed Huntly in the 1870s. Originally starting as a native school in 1896, the Te Wharekura O Rakaumanga Primary School was relocated to make way for the construction of the Huntly Power Station. In 1984, the school was one of the first in New Zealand to become bilingual (Māori/English). Then in 1994 became Kura Kaupapa where Māori is its first language.

New Zealand's largest thermal power station is located in Huntly. It is fuelled by gas and coal. The area is also known for its large coal deposits. The open cast coal mine is the second largest open cast mine in the country.

"Well," said Aroha, "we will have to find work somewhere; we are just about sweeping the bottom of the barrel."

"What is there to do in Huntly?" asked James. "I do miss the circus."

As they were close to entering the township, Aroha noticed fruit and veg outlets.

"I have an idea," said Aroha.

It was the second shop along the pathway where she enquired if there was any work for her and James. The owner was Chinese (Mrs Woo), she was very difficult to understand; however, Aroha did manage to ascertain that Mrs Woo was contemplating closing the shop for four days as she had to take her husband to hospital for a minor operation.

"You good with figures?" asked Mrs Woo. "If so, you work here four day with little brother," she said, pointing at James. "I pay you good after four day."

She showed Aroha where all the stock was stored, and to make sure the display stands were kept full. "I go now," said Mrs Woo, "you look after place good."

"We will," said Aroha, and with that Mrs Woo left to take her husband to the Waikato Hospital in Hamilton.

"Well, that was a bit of a whirlwind tour of the premises," Aroha said. And with that, customers were walking into the store. Fortunately, prices were displayed with the goods. Aroha was bagging up goods for customers. Meanwhile, James was busy bringing in stock from the storage and filling up depleted stands.

"What's that?" asked Aroha.

"A potato man," said James.

He made a large potato man using three large potatoes and placed it in the middle of the potato stand. A lot of the children that came in were quite amused and wanted to buy it, but the potato man was not for sale. They were so busy they didn't realise it was already after five p.m. when the store was supposed to close.

"I don't feel too confident in camping out with this till money. I have an idea," said James. "What if we stay overnight in the store? There is a kitchen, toilet and bathroom out the back."

"Good thinking," said Aroha, "I'll hide the money somewhere."

They decided to fill up all the stands in preparation for tomorrow.

"It's like living in a motel," said James, "better than in a tent."

Next morning, they opened up early about seven a.m. No sooner had the door been opened, customers were coming in. So many varieties of fruit and vegetables, Aroha was getting quite used to working out the costs according to the goods' weight. James was constantly replenishing. At last, a bit of a break, and James was able to rest for about three minutes. They were able to have a bite to eat and drink in-between customers. By the end of the day, they were exhausted. Cleaning up and re-stocking the stands, they declared the shop closed. After tea, they decided to go for a short walk around the shops. "That's enough walking," said

James. "I'm so tired carrying the produce, I think I'll go back."

Aroha agreed and they went back to their new accommodation for the night.

The next day was as busy as the day before and so was the fourth. Mrs Woo returned on that day early afternoon. She was so pleased with the efforts that Aroha and James put in that she paid them quite handsomely with a small bonus for their honesty. They told her that they stayed at the store each night. She allowed them to stay that night and they were off to Hamilton the next day. Getting all their things together, Mrs Woo gave them a large bag of fruit and bid them goodbye.

"She wasn't a bad old stick," said James.

"I think she was very nice," Aroha replied, "and quite generous."

Chapter 7
-37.828406,175.357307

Via Thermal Explorer Highway, they headed for Hamilton. Hamilton was settled by Europeans in 1864. It is named after Captain John Hamilton. After slow beginnings, it eventually claimed city status in 1945. The city is now the fourth largest in New Zealand.

The Waikato River is the longest river in the country. It flows past Hamilton and often referred to as The Mighty Waikato River. It stretches from the eastern hills of Mt Ruapehu and into the Tasman Sea south of Auckland. The river provides water not only for Hamilton city but a number of communities, towns and cities including Auckland.

Aroha and James found a small café in mid-city for their lunchtime break. Shops, people and cars everywhere, they felt as though they were back in Auckland. After a bit of a stroll, they decided to head out of the city and considered Tamahere on the outskirts of Hamilton a good place to set up camp. They found an area just short of Tamahere which provided shelter and privacy.

Highway 23 is a short stretch to Raglan on the coast. But both highways 39 and 3 just keep going and going until they meet up at Otoro....

Whilst they only recently earned money in Huntly, they decided there might be a good opportunity to get employment in Cambridge, maybe at some stables. The next morning, they set off for Cambridge which was only a sixteen-km ride.

"Where do you start?" said James. "There are so many horse places."

"They are called horse stables, not places," said Aroha. "We'll just have to go and ask," she said.

They went to a grand-looking property that looked a bit too posh for them to work in. Aroha asked one of the workers if there were any jobs available. He said he didn't know but to check with the manager who was in the tackle shed. They soon found the manager, he said there were no vacancies, but he knew the stable down the road was looking for some help.

"Just carry on for about one kilometre and it's the cream-coloured house on the left."

Aroha knocked on the door which was answered by a four-year-old girl (Sophie). "Is your mum or dad at home?" asked Aroha.

"I'll get Mummy," said Sophie. "Muuuuuummmmmmmm!" she shouted. "There's someone here."

Sophie's mother came to the door with both hands covered in a sticky dough. "Excuse me," she said, "but I am making some bread."

"That's OK," said Aroha, "we have just come to see if you have any jobs for us at your stables."

"You will need to ask my husband, he's next door in the garage."

"Thank you," said Aroha and James. They found the farmer working on his hot rod in the garage.

"What do you think of this?" he asked.

"Cooooool," said James.

"How can I help?" he went on.

Aroha said, "We were enquiring at the neighbours for stable work and were told that you may have a vacancy."

"I do," he said, "how much experience do you have."

"Well," James started, "none."

Aroha interjected, "But we are quick to learn."

"My name is Dave." Aroha and James introduced themselves. Dave said, "I will give you a try, but I must warn you, it's hard work."

"We are used to hard work," James blurted before he realised what he was saying.

Dave showed them around the stables at the back of the property. There was one worker cleaning out a stable who he introduced as Wendy. Wendy, in fact, trained the horses but because they were so short-staffed, she did the cleaning as well. Dave asked Wendy to show Aroha and James what to do and then went back to work on his hot rod. There were eight stables to clean out each day, horses to be fed and riding tackle to be cleaned. Wendy gave them permission to lodge in one of the empty stables.

They worked there for just over a week. James just couldn't help himself. After grooming one of the horses, he decided to get up on its back. The horse jolted forward, causing James to slip onto the horse's neck which he hung onto with all his strength whilst the horse trotted around the stables.

"I'm falling, I'm falling!" James cried. *Thud*, he hit the ground.

"Are you all right?" called Aroha as she raced over to him.

"Yes, I'll live," James replied.

"For goodness' sake, leave the horses alone," said Aroha in a stern manner.

James went back and carried on cleaning out the stable but kept his distance from the horses.

It was time to move on. Aroha went over to see Dave and mentioned that she and James needed to call this their last day as they had to be off on their journey the next morning. Dave thanked them for all their work and said they could still stay overnight in one of the stables. After they were paid, Aroha took James' pay to put with hers.

"Hey," he said, "don't take it all."

She gave him $5. "That's plenty of pocket money."

Next morning, they set off for their next destination Tīrau. They passed through Karāpiro. Lake Karāpiro is a manmade lake on the Waikato River. Whilst the lake was made for the purpose of providing water for the Karāpiro hydroelectric power station, it has also become a venue for world class water sport events.

"Did you know that it's only seven days until Christmas?" said James. "I love Christmas," he went on, "that's the time for giving AND receiving. I gave my friends paper darts last year, I'm pretty good at making them. I've never had a bought present given to me but you never know, one day."

Chapter 8
-37.976815,175.756324

As with previous destinations, the pair arrived at Tīrau just on lunchtime. Well, what is there to know about Tīrau. Tīrau (place of many cabbage trees) is a quirky town also known as the Corrugated Capital of the World. This is because of the number of large sculptures made of corrugated iron gracing the township. It is a major road junction, remaining on State Highway 1 will lead you to Taupō, whereas branching off onto Highway 5 will take you to Rotorua. The high traffic volume through the town brings with it a buyer's mecca to the number of antique, collectables and other niche retail outlets.

In addition to the remarkable sculptures stands a castle on a hill top. It was opened in 2000 as a museum; a toy museum. Toys, dolls, models, trains and various displays. Some of the dolls and toys date back to the 1800s. The castle has its own moat although gentle goldfish inhabit its waters.

As they had recently been paid, Aroha and James decided to dine out for lunch at one of the main street cafés. James didn't hold back on sausage rolls and chips. They spent much of the afternoon poring over nick nacks and memorabilia in a number of 'curiosity' shops.

"I think I'll buy one of these souvenir teaspoons," Aroha said. "It has welcome to Tīrau, and only costs fifty cents. It will remind me of our stay in Tīrau."

James didn't know what he wanted; first a book, then a fence wire strainer, bow and arrow, clock, hat, tea cup. "I want it all!" he shouted.

"Sssshhh," said Aroha, "everyone will look at us if they don't throw us out first."

James just couldn't make up his mind so walked out and into the next shop.

Crossing the road again for the fifth time, Aroha said, "What's going on over there?"

By the information centre, a crowd had gathered. They couldn't see very much from the back so James pushed his way in between the onlookers, he got to the front almost losing his balance then steadied himself in the open space just as the star of the show asked for a volunteer.

"Aha and here is a volunteer."

James was just about to say he was not volunteering when he was grabbed and manhandled onto a chair. "Let us demonstrate how to immobilise a person with multiple injuries."

Yes, James fell into the snare of a St John First Aid demonstration day educating the public on bandaging. Three St John members began weaving their web of bandage. One concentrated on the head, another the left leg and the third the right arm. When they had finished, James could hardly move; apparently, he had head injuries, a broken leg and broken arm.

"So, this is how you immobilise a patient's limbs and bandage a head wound," said the chief first aider. "Are there any questions?" she asked. "If not, work in pairs, take bandages from the box and see how you can effectively immobilise your partner's injured limbs." This was going on for about ten minutes when James said, "What about me?"

"Oh, I had forgotten all about you, I suppose we had better untie you."

"Free at last!" said James as he hurried over to Aroha. "Let's get out of here before someone else comes over looking for a patient," he mumbled.

They snuck behind the crowd planning their escape on the run until they reached the doors of another bric-a-brac shop. The day was drawing to a close so they decided to bike a short distance out of Tīrau to set up their camp site.

Next day, they headed to Tokaroa. Again, slightly further than they would have liked but thirty-two kilometres was not too far. After ten kilometres, they came to Putāruru. Its Blue Water Springs flow down from the Mamaku plateau, filtering water as it flows. Some 70% of New Zealand bottled water comes from the Blue Springs. Putāruru township also gets its water supply from the springs.

Eventually arriving in Tokoroa, just in time for a well-earned lunch break. Tokoroa is a town developed in 1917. Its significant forest areas made it a large timber-processing settlement. In addition, a pulp and paper mill was established, for the processing of timber from the large-scale pine forest plantations.

Throughout the town is a public art display. Known as Talking Poles, these are tall carved wooden structures (other materials are also used). There are over forty sculptures depicting the towns various cultures, clubs and organisations. The idea began in 1996, carving workshops were also held by the master carvers. After lunch, the pair decided to top up provisions at the local supermarket. From there, they travelled a further five kilometres to a suitable camp site.

Next morning, they travelled close to thirty kilometres. Due to the heavily forested areas on both sides of the road, it was not too difficult to find a suitable area to set up camp. They happened to be fairly close to Lake Ohakuri. Ohakuri is a dam and hydroelectric power station on the Waikato River.

The next day brought a beautiful sunny morning, they set off on a trip to the first major tourist resort, Taupō. The trip consisted of wide roads with significant forested areas on either side. They eventually arrived in Wairakei, a small settlement situated in an active geothermal area. In 1958, a geothermal electric power-generating station had been established using the natural energy resource to provide electricity. You know when you are nearing Wairakei, plumes of steam in the form of white clouds rise skyward from discharge vents.

Taupō (Taupō-nui-a-Tia) which translated relates to the explorer Tia, 'the great cloak of Tia'. Known for Lake Taupō, the largest freshwater lake in Australasia. The lake was formed about twenty-seven thousand years ago by an enormous volcanic eruption which caused a huge area of land to collapse. This resulted in a deep crater. The lake is fed by the Waitahanui, Tongariro, and Tauranga Taupō rivers. Taupō is a very popular tourist destination. Of the many tourist activities, sky diving, jet boating, paragliding and bungy jumping, to name only a few.

And the reports were right. There were lots and lots of tourists in and around the township, on the lake and in the air paragliding.

"What a super playground," James announced.

"Yes," replied Aroha, "it would be awesome to try out some of those activities."

After lunch, they went for a wander by the lake's edge.

"I have got to have a go at that," said James in a high-pitched exited voice. It was the hole in one challenge. One ball at $1.50.

"I'll take two," said James.

Standing high looking over the lake, a pontoon structure some a hundred and two metres from land floated in the lake. A red flag identified the position of the hole. Teed up the first ball, James acted like a pro, standing back and swinging the golf club. Then walking up to the tee, he took a swipe. The bottom of the club hit the top surface of the ball, making it dribble off the tee and rolling down the bank. That did not deter James. Placing the second ball on the tee, he took an enormous swing and missed the ball. The club slipped through his hands and flew out into the lake. He looked at the owner, the owner looked at James.

"You are supposed to hit the ball into the lake, not the club," said the owner, as his body language was beginning to show signs of significant annoyance.

"Oooops," said James, "I didn't mean to—"

Aroha held James by the arm and marched him away before any further altercation.

After they were some distance, James turned to Aroha. "Thank you for saving me, I thought he was going to throw me into the lake to get it back."

They sat on one of the seats along the lake's edge and watched all kinds of activity going on. As it was a fine day, they could see Mt Ruapehu in the distance.

"What an awesome sight," said Aroha. James nodded in agreement.

They decided to stay a night at a fairly cheap backpackers'. At $38, it wasn't too bad although they had to keep a good account of their outgoings being on such a strict budget. Aroha was good at keeping tabs on their money situation. If it were left to James, he would have spent it all in one day.

Next morning, they were on their way to Tūrangi. A beautiful scenic ride along the lake's edge.

Southward bound, where on earth does state highway 5 end up? Could it be Esk........

Tūrangi is some fifty kilometres, they thought it would be too far for one day's bike ride. After about thirty kilometres they decided to stop at one of several camps along the lake's edge. There were quite a few people at the camps, they befriended a family of six (parents and four children). They were invited for soccer games and then dinner in the evening.

"That was delicious," said Aroha, (they hadn't had a cooked meal of meat and vegies for ages).

"It's our pleasure," the parents replied.

Up at day break, they rode off to Tūrangi. A small town on the bank of the Tongariro River, Tūrangi is well-known for its trout fishing. Brown and Rainbow trout were introduced in the Tongariro River in the late nineteenth century. After lunch, they decided to travel further and at least get partially onto the Desert Road.

State Highway 47 and 46 join to 4 and if you branch off onto State Highway 43, that leads to a snow-capped mount Ruap....

After just four kilometres, they biked past the Tongariro National Trout Centre. The centre is managed by the Department of Conservation. The trout centre has a hatchery, an underwater viewing chamber, a museum and freshwater aquariums filled with native freshwater fish. A number of Whio (native blue duck) bred in captivity spend their early life in a specially built predator-proof sanctuary within the grounds. The ducklings stay in the facility during the summer months and then released when strong enough to fend for themselves.

Chapter 9
-39.481091,175.669900

In complete contrast to almost the rest of the country is the Rangipo Desert in the Ruapehu District. Its barren landscape was formed by volcanic activity some twenty thousand years ago. There is very little vegetation except for tussock and snow grasses. The barrenness is mainly due to the very-poor-quality soil. It has a high annual rainfall of 1.5 to 2.5 metres. Heavy snowfalls occur in the winter months, to the extent of requiring the road to be closed until snow can be cleared. Mounts Tongariro, Ngauruhoe and Ruapehu tower over the hundred square kilometre desert area, of which Mt Ruapehu is the highest peak.

The New Zealand army has its base in Waiouru to the south of the desert. The desert is used as a training area for the defence force. Of interest, some of the scenes of *The Lord of The Rings* were shot in the desert area.

With the Kaimanawa Range of mountains to the east, Rangipo Desert and the Kaimanawa ranges are also home to wild horses. Originally, the importation and crossing of Exmoor ponies with Welsh ponies in the nineteenth century, resulted in what were named Comet breed. Some were released in the wild and mixed with many other ponies and horses that had either escaped or released in the Kaimanawa area. The horses are of a solid stature and have a remarkably calm temperament.

Initially, the horse population increased significantly; however, with land development and sporting activities the herd numbers declined to only a hundred and seventy-four horses. A management program has been established to keep control of horse numbers. This has been prepared in order to protect the environment in which they roam and protect the wellbeing of the horses. The horse population has been kept at about three hundred.

"I wonder if we'll see any wild horses," said Aroha.

"I hope not," said James, "they might charge at us," (secretly thinking about his equestrian mishap in Cambridge).

"I don't think so," Aroha replied.

One went past, then another and another and another… They got off their bikes and watched a convoy of army trucks driving past. Eventually, the last one stopped.

"Where are you off to?" asked the driver.

"Waiouru," replied Aroha.

"Do you want a lift?"

"Yes, please," blurted James.

Two soldiers jumped from out the back of the truck, put the bikes in the back and lifted Aroha and James up onto the deck. There were another eight soldiers seated on either side.

"Well, where are you two off to?" asked the sergeant as she moved over to make room for James.

"We are on holiday," Aroha replied, "and biking the length of New Zealand, ending in Bluff."

"Well, that's quite an undertaking," the soldiers agreed, "it would probably be more demanding than the exercises we do here."

"We don't go too far each day," Aroha continued, "and sometimes we rest up for several days."

James asked if he could drive one of the army tanks, they all laughed.

"Maybe when you're older, you can join the army and then drive a tank," the sergeant said.

It didn't take too long when they arrived at Waiouru. Being helped off the very high truck deck and handed their bikes, they thanked the soldiers and continued on their way.

As well as Waiouru being a military training area, a major attraction is the National Army Museum which opened in 1978. It houses displays of military heritage and exhibitions. The imposing building is likened to a fortress with armoured tanks and guns at its entrance.

By turning right onto State Highway 49 and connecting to State Highway 4 travelling south, you can reach a city where you can board a paddle steamer along the river Whang.....

They had to travel at least five kilometres before they could find a suitable camp area due to the somewhat barren terrain. A bit further than they really wanted to go, but it would make the next day's travel that much easier with just over twenty kilometres to Taihape. Slightly later morning rise as they weren't in any major hurry, they headed towards Taihape.

"You know, it's Christmas Day tomorrow," James announced.

"How can I forget, you've mentioned it often enough," replied Aroha.

"Just thinking of you," James continued, "I thought I would keep you in the loop during this festive season."

Taihape is a small rural town servicing the local farming community and the many travellers passing through on State Highway 1. Due to its terrain, some five hundred metres above sea level, sheep and cattle are farmed in this hill country environment.

Taihape is famous for its gumboot throwing festival. Local business people came up with the concept of competitors throwing gumboots, where of course the furthest thrown proclaims the winner. The festival was first held on 9 April 1985 and has been held annually ever since. The town is often referred to as the Gumboot Capital of the World. The welcome sign of Taihape is a corrugated iron sculpture of a gumboot.

With the weather turning, they had to wear their ponchos. It was just a light drizzle but even so, they would have got quite wet without them.

"Maybe we should have stayed put until it stopped raining," said James.

Aroha thought about it a bit but replied, "Who knows how long this might last? Besides, it is fairly mild so we shouldn't get too cold."

They arrived in Taihape and decided to stay overnight a little out of the township. Before setting up camp, they had a wander around the town and popped into the information centre which was also the Taihape library. James led Aroha to the books, suggesting they have a short time perusing some editions, especially those with lots of pictures and very few words as far as James was concerned.

Aroha asked one of the assistants when does the gumboot throwing festival take place.

"That's not until March," the lady said, "in about two and a half months."

Aroha was a bit disappointed that she couldn't take part in the fun activity. They left the information centre and rode off to a secluded area off the road. It was still drizzling and putting up tents in the rain wasn't too much fun. At least, it was quite dry inside the tent.

"It's Christmas Day!" came the shout from James' tent very early morning.

"Is it really?" came a voice from Aroha's tent. James scurried over to Aroha's tent excitedly with a present he had wrapped up the night before. Aroha had a wrapped gift for James which he snatched from her, ripping up the wrapping. It was a large caramel milk chocolate bar.

"My favourite!" mumbled James with a mouthful of chocolate. "Go on," he said, handing Aroha a gift, "open it."

Aroha carefully unwrapped the present and with a forced smile said thank you for the tube of toothpaste.

"You said you were running out, so that gave me a clue what you really wanted." Hesitantly, James broke off a piece of chocolate for Aroha, not too much though as he wanted the bar for himself.

The grey day still brought with it a fine drizzle but they decided to carry on. They had no option but to put the soaking wet tents into their backpacks. It was Mangaweka, this time only twenty kilometres' ride. A feature in Mangaweka is a DC-3 plane by the highway which is utilised as a café. The aircraft and surrounding area are closed due to redevelopment.

Again, due to its steep terrain, a number of large railway viaducts span high over river valleys. The Makohine Viaduct has a category 1 listing as a heritage site.

Fortunately, the rain had stopped and with the skies clearing, the sun made for a very warm day.

"Just what we need," said Aroha.

Rather than the side of the road, the pair decided to go to the Mangaweka camping grounds. The tent sites being right beside the Rangitikei River surrounded by high cliffs, what an awesome sight! Aroha suggested they empty their backpacks and spread out all the damp items for drying.

Next morning began a slightly longer trip to Hunterville, some twenty-seven kilometres. On biking about fifteen kilometres, they came to a rest stop on the other side of the road. Waiting for traffic to pass, they crossed over. From the rest stop looking back, they saw the impressive Makohine Viaduct high in the hills.

From the rest stop, it was only a further twelve kilometres to Hunterville. The famous welcome sign of Hunterville is a statue of a huntaway dog. These dogs have been bred in New Zealand since the nineteenth century. They are a strong, hardy dog that can better cope with the hill country terrain. On a day in October, Hunterville hosts the annual event known as Shepherds' Shemozzle. This festival calls for shepherds from around the country to compete in a gruelling cross-country and obstacle race partnered with their huntaway dog.

James was getting quite tired. "When are we going to have a break from biking?" he asked. "We have been on the road nonstop since Huntly."

"You're right," agreed Aroha. "We will stop for a break at the next town where we can get work. We are running out of money, so we need to get some employment fairly soon."

They arrived at Hunterville, set up and had a fairly early night for their next trip to Bulls.

They set off early morning. Bulls is named after James Bull who had established a general store in the area. Residents and business owners have made light of the town name by slightly altering names and words to end with the word bull. And that's not all; to add to this clever wackiness, the township of Bulls has joined with its sister city Cowes, England. What do you think of these creations, just to name a few:

Chiropractic clinic — Adjust-a-Bull

Florist — Bloom-a-Bulls

Fire Brigade — Extinguish-a-Bull

Pharmacy — Indispens-a-Bull

Historical Society — Memor-a-Bull

House Movers — Transport-a-Bull

"I doubt we will get employment here," said Aroha, "as we are probably not employ-a-Bull."

"Oh, very funny," said James. "Well, let's get to Palmerston North and see if that will be work-a-Bull."

The following morning, they set off for Palmerston North. Only a couple of kilometres after leaving Bulls, they passed a signpost Ohakea, Royal New Zealand Air Force Base. Due to its long runway, it acts as a take-off and landing strip for both military and civilian aircraft.

They biked through Sanson, some four kilometres past Ohakea. Eventually, they arrived in Palmerston North City. "I need something edi-Bull and drink-a-Bull," said James.

"I think that's enough Bull for one day," replied Aroha.

After lunch and a bit of a wander, they biked a little out of the city and found a place to set up camp. Then back into town towards evening. It was New Year's Eve and they decided to join in the celebrations. The show started at six p.m. at The Event Quadrant, The Square.

"This is awesome!" said James.

As the day was getting darker, there started laser and stroboscopic lighting effects during the various acts, magic shows, music and dancing,

"This is great!" said Aroha. "I have never been to a New Year's party. I'll be going every year from now on."

And finally, the main event, the Countdown. Party goers shouted down the numbers... "3, 2, 1, HAPPY NEW YEAR!" With that at the stroke of twelve, a huge fire work display filled the night sky with all manner of coloured lights, and the air filled with spent gunpowder smoke. 2019 had dawned. Aroha and James biked off to their camp, ready for bed and a sleep-in.

With January 1 and 2 being statutory holidays, the pair had to bide their time from looking for employment. This gave a great opportunity to have a look around the city. Relatively flat terrain allowed them to venture out of town, which included a bit of a tour in and around Massey University campus.

The next day, it didn't take long for Aroha to find work at a florist's. Sue was in need of a helping hand

and was delighted when Aroha asked for a job. Aroha was shown how to take phone orders, ensuring accurate contact and address details. In between orders, she would strip thorns and dead foliage from flower stems, prepare buckets with water and some flowers needing to be refrigerated. Aroha was also responsible for keeping work benches tidy and sweeping the floors. On her feet most of the time made for quite an exhausting day. The next day, Sue allowed Aroha to try her hand at making a small posy bowl. After a number of attempts and suggestions from Sue, Aroha finally made a creation that she was quite proud of; and even more ecstatic when someone purchased it a couple of hours later.

James managed to get a job close by, at a car sales, washing cars.

"See all those cars at the back?" the manager said to James. "I want them all sparkling clean."

James was handed a bucket, a sponge, car wash liquid, a hose and drying cloths. James was overwhelmed with the number of cars. Maybe continuing biking was a better option, he thought, but they had to earn some money somehow.

After three days, they decided to move on. The intention was to get to Woodville through the Manawatū Gorge and then onto Pahiatua. They found out, however, that the Gorge was closed and the only way was over the Pahiatua Track. It's a thirty-kilometre trip, something they were reasonably used to for a day cycling but they didn't realise the steepness of the road.

"I can't bike up this," said Aroha, "it's just too steep." She got off and walked, with James following suit half a minute later.

It was a steep climb, the road passing through the Tararua Mountain Range. After walking, resting and walking again, they got to the top. Whilst there were a number of ups and downs, they eventually got to the part of the track which was predominantly downhill.

"Well," said James, "that was a bit of an ordeal, I hope we don't strike any more of those climbs." (*I had better not mention to them at this point so they don't get too disheartened, but there is worse to come after about a hundred kilometres' travel*).

They eventually arrived in Pahiatua, a rural service town for the mainly beef, sheep and dairy farming in the area. As well as its agriculture, two large manufacturing plants are located just out of the township. The Fonterra Dairy Factory producing milk and milk powder products and the Tui Brewery where the brewing of beer began in 1889. Pahiatua also has its own regional television station known as Tararua Television. It has viewers throughout the Manawatū-Whanganui region.

During World War II, New Zealand decided to accept child refugees from Poland, and in 1944, seven hundred and thirty-three children arrived in Wellington. A refugee camp was set up about two kilometres south of Pahiatua. The camp was only meant to be a temporary home for the children. However, they stayed on until 1949, when they were naturalised New Zealand citizens.

After that trek, the pair were exhausted so finding a place to camp and relaxing for the rest of the afternoon was top of the list.

The next morning was overcast with rain threatening, but they took the risk and ventured down to Eketāhuna. A small rural service town, it was initially settled by Scandinavian immigrants who named the town Mellemskov (heart of the forest). By the late 1870s, the town name was changed to the Māori name Eketāhuna (meaning — to run aground on a sand bank), which describes the area where their canoes (*waka*) were unable to travel further along the Mākākahi River.

The threatening rain saw clouds begin to retreat, larger areas of blue sky made way for sunshine. "Just as well we took the risk," said Aroha. James agreed. After some ten kilometres, they arrived at the Pūkaha National Wildlife Centre, in the Mt Bruce area. Established in 1962, the then-55-hectare centre was set up to breed and release endangered native birds. In 2001, the entire surrounding forest area was added to the centre, bringing the protective expanse up to a huge 942 hectares. In addition to the endangered bird species, the centre also breed and display, reptiles, aquatic animals and invertebrates, not to mention the reptilian Tuatara. The Tuatara is the only surviving species of the Sphenodontia that lived about one hundred and eighty million years ago. The Tuatara is only found in New Zealand, it has an average life span of fifty to sixty years.

BUT WAIT, there's more. New Zealand is also home to an animal that has become an icon of the country; the kiwi (hidden bird). The kiwi is a flightless bird that is active and hunts at night. They are related to the now extinct moa (found only in New Zealand), and Australian emus and cassowaries. Its unusual features include nostrils at the end of its beak, no tail, loose hair-like feathers that moult during the year and it has whiskers. Kiwi are also bred at the wildlife centre.

James noticed a mob of sheep being herded close by.

"Come on," he said, "I have an idea." They stopped at the side of the road and James asked the farmer what was he up to. He told them the sheep were just a number of stragglers for shearing and as there were not too many, he was going to shear them himself rather than get a gang of shearers. James asked if there was any chance of a job for himself and Aroha.

The farmer said, "You are a blessing in disguise. I was wondering how I was going to do this on my own."

James and Aroha would be employed as shed hands. The farmer (Joel) said, "It will only be for a couple of days."

"That would be awesome," James replied.

"Well, if you are ready," Joel said, "you can start right now."

They herded the sheep into covered holding yards, got the shearing shed in order for the next day's shear. Joel allowed the pair to stay overnight at the shearers' quarters.

"This will save us setting up our tents," James whispered to Aroha.

The following day, Joel began shearing. Aroha and James were putting the fleece into wool bales and sweeping Joel's shearing area clear. At the end of the second day, the shearing was completed and the three were quite exhausted. Joel came back later that evening and gave them their pay. "Thanks very much for your help," he said and wished them well on their journey for the next day.

The following day, they set off for Masterton. "That was a good idea of yours for getting that extra work and pay," said Aroha. "It will help pay for tickets for the ferry from Wellington to Picton."

Now here is something a little bit interesting. Did you know that Masterton is the exact antipode (the parts of the earth diametrically opposite) of Marazoleja in Spain. What is the antipode of the area that you live?

Masterton is the largest town of the Wairarapa District. Joseph Masters after whom the town is named was spokesperson of the committee which secured the purchase of land with the government. The land purchase helped form the town.

Masterton is also home to the Golden Shears competition. The sheep shearing competition began in

1961 and international championships are now held each year during March.

As they were entering Masterton township, they turned right into Oxford Street to the Mawley Holiday Park where they were able to set up camp for the night. After pitching their tents, they rode off into town. There were hundreds of people gathering at Queen Elizabeth II Park (Masterton's main park). James went over to a group of people and enquired as to what was happening. The crowds were getting ready to compete for the colour fun run.

"Can we go on that?" asked James.

"It looks like fun. I think we can afford this," said Aroha. She went to the marquee to register.

They were given a small goodie bag with a pack of colour powder. The total loop was six kilometres, but competitors were able to choose a small, medium or long loop.

"Shall we take the medium loop?" asked Aroha.

"Yes, that would be good," replied James. "I think the long loop would be too far."

They only just got there in time; no sooner did they get to the start area when all of a sudden, they were off. Some competitors just couldn't wait showering and being showered by nontoxic coloured powder right from the start. Aroha and James were wearing sunglasses and hats as was recommended by the organisers. At various points, organisers were powdering competitors as they ran past. The competitors all congregated in one area at the end of the run where there was a humongous showering of coloured powder. Red, yellow, green, pink, blue. Aroha and James were absolutely covered, unrecognisable beneath the coloured disguise.

"This is great!" said James. They rode back to the camp grounds, had showers, used the laundry for their rainbow-coloured clothes and went for a bit of a wander around the grounds.

The next morning, they decided on Greytown as their next destination. As they headed out of Masterton, Aroha pointed up into the sky. They stopped on the side of the road to watch. Six sky divers jumped from a plane. They watched the freefall lasting about thirty seconds and then several minutes of gently parachuting down. The drop zone (where parachutists land) is within the Hood Aerodrome area, the site from where the plane originally took off.

"I wish I could do that," said James.

"Too scary for me," replied Aroha, "jumping out of a plane some ten thousand feet high."

They arrived in Carterton, a small town which was founded in 1857. Named after Charles Carter who held a number of government positions and was on the committee of the Wairarapa Small Farms Association. He was responsible for the settlement of Masterton and Greytown and, subsequently, Carterton.

The self-claimed Daffodil Capital of New Zealand in 1995, Carterton has each year held a daffodil carnival which includes market stalls, the "Daffodil Express" steam train bringing visitors from Wellington and, of course, daffodil picking on Middle Run Farm along Gladstone Road. A wave of brilliant yellow stretching as far as the eye can see, and then crowds appearing ready to gather the bright coloured flowers. Proceeds from the event are donated to charity organisations.

Another ten kilometres and they arrived in Greytown. Turning right into Kuratawhiti Street, they found the camping ground which forms part of the Greytown Park. As there weren't any little kids around at the time, Aroha and James had a quick turn on the swings and slides in the park's play area.

Greytown was first settled on 27 March 1854. As with Masterton and Carterton, it was developed under the Small Farms Association Settlement Scheme. The town was named after Governor Grey who supported the settlement scheme.

As a result of some persuasive conservationists, Arbour Day (a day set aside for conservation tree planting which occurs in many countries) was held in Greytown in 1854. It was the first Arbour Day celebration in New Zealand. Arbour Day continues to be celebrated each year with many schools in partnership with government initiatives take part in tree planting.

The Papawai Marae located in Pah Road just outside of Greytown's town centre is one of the most important maraes in the country. Its importance is mainly attributable to its historic past. In the late 19 century, it became the meeting place of the Māori Parliament. Interestingly, carved figures around the marae face inward as a mark of peace contrary to outward-facing figures representing a challenge.

Next morning, they set off for Upper Hutt, close to forty-three kilometres but as they were well-rested, they thought they would attempt that distance. *(Do you remember me saying there was worse to come about a hundred kilometres ago? Well, it's not far now)*. The pair arrived in Featherston.

A small town the furthest south in the Wairarapa. Over recent years, it has become a popular town for people from Wellington to relocate. Mainly due to the cheaper housing prices, and ease for commuting with its close proximity to the metropolitan cities of the Hutt Valley and Wellington.

Just some seven kilometres south of the township is Lake Wairarapa. The lake is part of a large lake/wetland system and known as Wairarapa Moana. Evidence shows that the area has been settled in the 14 Century.

Only three kilometres to the north was the Featherston Military camp. It was established as a military training base during World War I with facilities to house several thousand soldiers. During World War II, it was converted to a prisoner of war camp where some eight hundred Japanese prisoners were held captive. There was an unfortunate incident on 25

February 1943 where a number of prisoners refused to work. A high-rank Japanese officer was wounded which led to a riot within the camp. New Zealand soldiers opened fire which resulted in forty-eight prisoners killed and over seventy wounded. Also, one New Zealand soldier died from gunshot wounds. A memorial garden has been established on the site.

Featherston also has a museum that houses a Fell engine. It is the only remaining Fell locomotive in the world. From 1878, the locomotive was used to pull carriages over the Remutaka Hill known as the Incline, to a height of 265 metres, carrying passengers from Upper Hutt to Cross Creek (Featherston). The train required specially fitted wheels that grip a raised centre rail to allow for braking. In 1955, a rail tunnel through the mountain range was opened. This in turn ended the seventy-seven-year operation of the incline railway.

Diverting onto state highway 53 will take you to the small rural town of Martinb.....

After a short break in Featherston, the pair ventured off on what is known as the Remutaka Hill Road, albeit part of State Highway 2. It was a gradual incline; after only one kilometre, they came to what looked like a layby which is known as Otauira Reserve. They stopped there and with his jaw dropped almost to the ground, James looked up towards the sky and made out the route of the road where he saw vehicles negotiating the steep winding road.

"Do we have to go up there to get to Upper Hutt?" he asked.

When you couldn't imagine a jaw dropping any further, you would swear Aroha's jaw was actually scraping the road. "I don't believe it!" she exclaimed.

According to a shop keeper in Featherston pointing out the direction to Upper Hutt, you had to go over the Remutaka Hill. When the pair had heard the word hill, they were anticipating a small hill, not Mount Everest. Well, there was not much they could do but to tread the road on foot. A slow arduous walk in a single file as the road was fairly narrow in parts and with heavy trucks passing in both directions made for very little room. The Remutaka Hill Road peaks at its summit some five hundred and fifty-five metres. It is part of the Remutaka Mountain Range which joins with the Tararua Range to the north. After about four kilometres of uphill tramp, they decided to call it a day and looked for a place to set up camp.

Chapter 10
-41.114725,175.231950

A slow start next morning at the very thought of walking up the mountain. At least, it was a fine day. James led the way, staying close to the road's edge, with Aroha trying to put up with the moans and groans coming from the front.

"I have to have a rest," said James after about three kilometres' climb. They came to a widened area where they were safe to rest up. "I need a muesli bar," James said rummaging through his backpack. He found two bars for himself and Aroha. "Onward and upward," said James, as if he were a commander-in-chief giving orders.

Two further kilometres had passed. "Look!" said James. "I think I can see the top." Their pace quickened, and after two hundred metres, they were there.

"We made it, we made it!" exclaimed James, crossing over the road to the summit rest area.

"What a view!" said Aroha. "It's like being on top of the world."

They decided to have lunch and a bit of a break before the next journey. A number of people stopped at the summit to admire the view and take photos. They got ready for their downhill flight. Aroha surveyed the steepness and warned James not to go too fast and keep brakes lightly on. He acknowledged the advice and down they went. Brakes had to be applied every so often; otherwise, they wouldn't be able to negotiate the winding corners. It didn't take very long at all until they got to the bottom. A further sixteen kilometres and they arrived in Upper Hutt.

Upper Hutt (Orongomai) lies in the Hutt Valley. It is one of four cities that make up the Wellington Metropolitan area. Having a wander through the shopping mall, they bought the necessity of life — an ice cream each, of course, with the added chocolate flake. Negotiating the traffic through town, they headed towards a holiday park which is located by the Hutt River. There they set up camp and spent the rest of the day relaxing after the ordeal of the Remutaka climb.

Consulting their map, they agreed they should try for Wellington; still some thirty-six kilometres, they were anxious to complete the North Island journey. Fortunately, they encountered a fairly flat road compared to the previous ups and downs.

A few kilometres past Upper Hutt, you can access State Highway 58 which will take you to the western coastline and about five kilometres from the city of Pori....

They rode past the turnoff to Lower Hutt; Lower Hutt (Te Awa Kairangi ki Tai) as with Upper Hutt is a city in the Wellington Region and part of the Wellington metropolitan area. It is the sixth largest city and is separated from Wellington by the Wellington harbour.

Entering the expressway, they were able to divert close to the railway line onto a cycle track. The still waters of the harbour glistened in the morning sunshine.

"I can see for miles," said Aroha; a ferry turning in from the Wellington Heads, a cruise ship berthed at the shipping terminal, a plane seen taking off from Wellington airport, travellers by air and sea and of course land by way of a motorway and railway terminating at the city centre.

Wellington (Te Whanganui-a-Tara) is the capital city of New Zealand. First settled by Europeans in 1839, it was declared the capital city in 1865, transferred from Auckland. Being the country's political centre, it includes a number of government institutions. At the southern tip of the North Island, Wellington is separated from the South Island by the Cook Strait (Te Moana-o-Raukawa). The Strait lies between the Tasman Sea and the South Pacific Ocean. A ferry service runs between Wellington and Picton (South Island).

Reaching the end of the cycle track, they had to turn off onto the road to Thorndon as cyclists where not allowed on the motorway which was a continuation of the expressway. They noticed a sign indicating the Interislander Ferry. Stopping on the side of the road, they re-evaluated their journey.

"Whilst I was looking forward to looking around Wellington, do you think we should catch the ferry now that we are by the terminal?" asked Aroha.

"I think that is a good idea," replied James. "I would also have liked to explore some of Wellington but the sea looks so calm and hopefully I won't get sea sick, so let's go now." It was just ten a.m.; the next sailing was twelve noon. After being helped with securing the bikes in the vehicle deck, they went to the upper passenger decks.

"Doesn't it look plush?" James said.

Food was available, there was a cinema on board plus lots of places to sit both inside and outside in the fresh air.

"Let's go outside," said James.

It was absolutely beautiful as the ship quietly left the terminal and made its way to the South Island. They were looking at the pockets of land around about, some of them being farmed, when all of the sudden, James cried out, "Look!" He raced to the end of the ship and around the corner. "Aha! There you are," he said as he turned the corner, being greeted by a startled parent with a baby in a pram which she held on to. "Oh, I'm sorry," said James.

Aroha had reached James by then. "Whatever are you doing?" she asked.

"I am so sure I saw a dog's tail vanishing around this corner. You haven't seen a dog go past here, have you?" James asked the parent.

"No," she said, "there hasn't been anything here, only me and my baby."

James apologised again for startling her.

"You haven't got over Timmy, have you?" said Aroha.

"I'm sure I saw his tail," said James, "so sure…" They went inside for lunch.

After lunch, they again went on the outer deck, leaning over the railing and looking into the deep blue sea. "Look," said James, "dolphins."

Five dolphins were frolicking over the waves of the ship's wake; a spectacular view of these acrobatic and energised mammals, and then they were gone.

"Wasn't that just something?" said James.

Aroha agreed, "I have never seen dolphins in real life and so close," she said.

Sailing through the Marlborough Sounds seemed so peaceful. The sounds were originally formed by glacial activity where the glacier carves out valleys which are flooded by the Cook Strait. The four Sounds that make up the cluster of Marlborough Sounds are Queen Charlotte, Kenepuru, Pelorus, and Mahau sounds. At the head of Queen Charlotte sound is the port of Picton where the ferries berth. The ferry eventually tied alongside the port; they had arrived in Picton.

On leaving the ship, they biked out from the terminal to the township. Turning around the corner on London Quay, they came to the war memorial. The memorial commemorates the lives lost in World Wars I and II. Walking under the memorial arch, they came to a grass recreation area and beyond that, a sandy shore to the glistening waters. What an awesome sight, towering hills meeting the water edge.

Picton (Waitohi) and the capital city Wellington connect State Highway 1 and the railway network via the ferry service. The book *The Voyage* by Katherine Mansfield was a short story written by her depicting her travel on the Cook Strait ferry from Wellington to spend some time with her grandparents in Picton.

The *MS Mikhail Lermontov*, a cruise ship, left Australia on its way for a cruise around New Zealand. On 16 February 1986, it hit rocks and sank. The wreck lies at Port Gore close to Picton and is now utilised for scuba diving training and recreation.

Chapter 11
-41.508954,173.959533

Aroha and James decided to stay at the Whatamango camping grounds. Despite being a further ten kilometres, it was reputed to be a good camp run by the Conservation Department. The camp site is located by the beach of Whatamango Bay and amongst the picturesque bush-clad hills.

Next day was the start of a fairly lengthy stint to Blenheim. Their decision mainly to get some berry-picking work.

They could have veered west towards State Highway 6 where there is much to see, joining up with highway 1 in Inverc……..

Initially, a steady climb, then from the brow a gentle descent that saw them through to Blenheim. It is a bit hilly but flattens out the closer they got to Blenheim. They stopped at Tuamarina, a small settlement for a break and early lunch. Another hour and ten kilometres later saw the pair arrive in Blenheim.

Blenheim (Waiharakeke, translated as Flax Stream) initially referred to as 'The Beaver' due to the water-logged terrain of the area. It was renamed in honour of the Battle of Blenheim (1704) in Bavaria. Its shingle, free-draining soils make ideal soil types for grape growing. Blenheim lies within the Marlborough region; the region has become the largest wine-producing area in the country. Its Sauvignon Blanc wine, a speciality of Blenheim, has proven international acclaim.

Just a few kilometres from the township is the Woodbourne Airport. It serves both as a domestic airport and Royal New Zealand Air Force base, primarily used for training new recruits and officer training. The training for trades is also carried out at the base.

A significant horticulture and viticulture region, with large apricot, apple and cherry orchards in addition to a variety of berry fruit farms and grapes for the wine industry.

"Surely, we will find some berry-picking work here," said James.

They went to the information centre and enquired about berry fruit picking.

"It's getting a bit late in the season," said the lady behind the counter, "but I think they are still looking for pickers at the blueberry farm. It's about three kilometres out of the township, you can try there," she said.

They left to search for the blueberry farm, although didn't need to do too much searching as the lady had drawn them a map to follow. As they rode out into the country, they were amazed at the sight of rows upon rows of grape vines as far as the eye can see. Blenheim is, of course, one of New Zealand's major wine-producing areas. They didn't have to bike too far when they found the orchard. So many fruit trees and berry varieties.

They made their way to the packing sheds and asked to speak with the boss. He was in the office keeping an eye on production via computer. Aroha asked if there were any jobs going, they were hoping for about one week of work.

"What are you good at?" asked Rupert (the boss).

"Any type of picking," Aroha said, "we have been picking strawberries but quick to learn picking other fruit."

"I'll give you a go; you have to be fast and you have to do it properly."

"We will," said Aroha.

"OK then, be here by seven a.m."

James nearly fainted at the thought.

"Can we pitch our tents on your property so that we don't have far to travel?" Aroha asked.

"Yes, that should be OK," said Rupert. "Behind those trees there, will that be OK?"

"Excellent," said Aroha.

"OK," replied Rupert and he went back to the office.

"OK, OK, how many more times is he going to say 'OK'?" asked James. They set up camp behind a small plantation of oak trees.

Next day, a very early start, Sally drove past on a tractor, pulling a large wooden trailer.

"All aboard," she called and some fifteen pickers (including Aroha and James) climbed on. They travelled on some narrow tracks to the lower part of the farm. There before them was a huge plantation of blueberries.

"Right, so some of you are new to this so I will repeat the process. It will also be a reminder to those that have done this before."

They were all given a plastic container attached to a belt; which was secured at waist height. She then showed them how to pick blueberries. "Stand up close to the plant, gently support a bunch of blueberries beneath the bunch and with your thumbs just roll or rub onto the berries. The ripe berries will fall off and by standing close to the plant, the berries will fall into the plastic container."

They all went through this process with Sally's eagle eye watching every movement. Once they got the hang of it, they emptied their containers into large trays on the trailer. James tried one, he had never tasted a blueberry before. Then another and another and a handful.

"STOP!" said Aroha. "Do you remember what happened at the strawberry farm?"

James cast his mind back and he could physically feel the stomach pain he had back then. That was the last blueberry for the day.

As they were picking, James overheard a group speaking a foreign language.

"I wonder where they are from," he whispered to Aroha.

"Don't be nosey," she said. "You better concentrate on picking before Sally sees you talking too much."

James carried on picking, when one of the group walked past him. James couldn't help himself. "Where are you from?" he enquired.

"We are from Zlín in the Czech Republic."

"Where's the Czech Republic?" James asked.

"It's in the centre and east of Europe. It borders Austria, Germany, Poland and Slovakia," the man replied.

"I am James, what's your name?"

The man replied, "Jiri, and these are my friends that have accompanied me to New Zealand; Marta, Trudy, Oskar and Petr."

"Nice to meet you all, this is Aroha."

Jiri explained that they were students and on a world trip for about a year, a sort of working holiday. "Can you teach me some Czech words?" asked James. "What's the word for 'hi'?"

"*Ahoj*," said Jiri.

"And 'good day'?"

"*Dobry den*," was the reply.

"And what about these berries, what are they called?"

"*Boruvka*," Jiri replied.

"That's fantastic!" said James. "I can now speak Czech; *ahoj*, this is a *boruvka*."

"Well done," said Jiri, "you catch on very quickly. The word *ahoj* can be used as a greeting and also saying goodbye like 'see you'."

"*Ahoj,*" said James. They went back to work before Sally had a chance to reappear.

James and Jiri struck up a bit of a friendship; during lunchtime breaks, talking about their New Zealand adventure and Jiri describing their world adventure.

"One day, I am going to travel the world," said James. "I will visit every country in existence."

After five days, Aroha and James decided on continuing their journey. James called out *ahoj* to Jiri and his friends and they set off for Seddon.

Seddon is a small town named after former Prime Minister Richard Seddon. It lies in the Awatere Valley. In the main, Seddon initially relied on its farming economy; however, similar to Blenheim, it moved to the grape-growing industry.

The next day was a trip to Ward about twenty-one kilometres; on the way, they passed Lake Grassmere (Kāpara-te-hau — wind-blown lake). Lake Grassmere is a shallow lake close to the open sea and is now used for salt production. Salt water is pumped into the lake and due to idyllic weather conditions in the region, very little rain and hot drying winds causing evaporation is the perfect process for salt production. As the lake dries out, salt crystals are formed which are harvested for processing.

They stopped on the side of the road overlooking the wetlands at the forefront of the lake; it was time to have a morning tea snack. No sooner had they set off again that Aroha stopped suddenly and got off her bike. Stooping over the road and walking fairly quickly whilst the traffic was clear, she caught this little feathered creature.

"What have you got?" called James, wondering what Aroha was up to.

She walked over to James with her hands cupped, gradually opening them to reveal a small fantail bird. It didn't have any obvious injury; quite likely hit a car, causing it to be a bit dazed. James took his warm new beanie that he hadn't yet worn from out of the backpack and they put the bird gently inside to make it feel secure and comfortable. An injured bird needs a quiet, calm environment to recover. "I think we will just sit here and wait to see what happens."

Fortunately, they had stopped by a wide grass area off the road.

"*Ahoj*, do you want some *boruvka*?" James asked the bird. "It might understand Czech more than English."

Aroha looked at him and with a sigh of *I think he's gone around the bend*, the fantail started to chirp quietly. The chirps started getting louder.

"I told you he can understand Czech," and putting his face close to the bird, "*Dobry den!*" he exclaimed. The bird chirped louder and louder.

"I think he might be well enough to let him go," said Aroha. They gently tipped the bird out from the beanie onto the grass. The bird flapped its wings, jumping into the air, eventually taking flight. Up it soared and then showing off with amazing acrobatics as fantails do, it vanished from sight.

"What a lovely little bird," said Aroha, picking up James' beanie. "Oops, I think it made a little poop in it."

"What!" said James, turning the beanie inside out and wiping it on the grass. "That's the last time I'll use my clothes for an animal, or bird, or fish or anything."

They came to the Ward Domain. Cycling in, they went to the Ward memorial shaped as a small pyramid and sited in the centre of a lawn area. It is known as the Flaxbourne Fallen Soldiers Memorial.

They came to a large hedgerow just before the township. Clambering over the fence and lifting their bikes over, they made their camp behind the foliage. Poring over the map, they decided the next ride as a fairly lengthy trip; some forty-two kilometres to the township of Clarence.

A fine morning, they made off early. Just a few kilometres into their journey and there before them was the ocean; that will be the main vista for the next hundred kilometres' cycling. With just a mild breeze, the sea was so calm that it looked like a sheet of glass reflecting the bright sunshine.

"Doesn't that look awesome?" said Aroha, "I would love to have a swim, though probably a bit too cold this early."

It was about halfway to Clarence when they arrived at a store. An ideal place to buy an ice cream. With their ice cream in one hand, steering the bike with the other, they carried on just a couple of hundred metres to better access to the seashore. How beautiful it was sitting on the beach gazing at the horizon; however, not without some pesky seagulls getting closer and closer, waiting for a chance to steal any part of the ice cream.

They found some sticks. Using one as a pencil, Aroha drew a huge shape of a horse that covered several square metres.

"I can do better than that," said James, so he started drawing.

"What's that?" asked Aroha.

"Can't you see?" said James. "It's a bird in flight."

"A bird?" Aroha quizzed. "I've never seen a bird like that before."

To be brutally honest, it looked more alien than any creature on this planet. At least, James was proud of his masterpiece. They started off again, another twenty kilometres and they arrived in Clarence. A small settlement, it is named after King William IV, who prior to his accession was Duke of Clarence.

An overnight stay and they were headed to Kaikoura; another forty-plus kilometres; although they did agree if it felt too much, they would make camp partway through. They travelled for twenty-five kilometres.

"What a lot of surfers!" exclaimed James.

It was a sea of surfers (*Did you get the pun?*). They had arrived in Mangamaunu which is famous for its ideal surfing environment. "I wish I could have a go at surfing," said James, "it looks pretty easy."

"It might look easy," replied Aroha, "but I bet it takes heaps of practice to get the balance right. If you attempted surfing, I would expect that I would be pulling you out of the water to save you from drowning."

"I don't think so," said James, "I'll prove it to you one day."

Today was not to be that day.

Chapter 12
-42.399406,173.679521

The next day was just a fifteen kilometre ride to Kaikoura (meal of crayfish). An awesome coastline where the Kaikoura Range (part of the southern alps) meets the Pacific Ocean. A large whaling industry was established in 1843 and continued for some hundred and twenty years, ending in 1964. Since then, the depleted whale population was protected and the area is now within the Southern Hemisphere Whale Sanctuary. Today, Kaikoura operates as a tourist resort. The main attractions include whale watching, observing orca and Southern fur seals and even swimming with the dolphins.

"I have never seen such awesome scenery," said James, "snow-capped mountains so close to the ocean."

"Quite spectacular!" replied Aroha.

They arrived in the township and decided to have a light morning tea at a café. They set off south just out of the township to Paia Point where they were able to set up camp right beside the beach. Hidden from the road by a row of trees and flaxes made for an ideal camp site.

"Look," James called, "more dolphins."

They watched the acrobatic quintet display a free show.

"I can watch them all day," said Aroha. "Aren't they just beautiful?"

They went for a walk along the beach and searched for marine life in the many rock pools.

They headed for Hundalee, only a twenty-kilometre ride. They left the scenic ocean view, but only for a while to reappear again in about a hundred kilometres. Hundalee is a rural locality by the Conway River. It was a railway terminus between 1939—1980. The station building was relocated to Waipara and now known as the Waikari station for the Weka Pass Railway. Setting up quickly, they just made it before it started raining. Another book-reading afternoon confined in their tents.

The morning saw the rain easing a little although they did wear their waterproof ponchos. Fortunately, the temperature made for a fairly mild day. A longer bike ride covering thirty-five kilometres to Cheviot was the order of the day despite James' moaning of wanting a rest every fifteen minutes.

Aroha couldn't take it any more; after about an hour's bike ride, she stopped on the side of the road next to a wide clearing. "Come on," she said, "you can have your rest and a bite to eat."

That was music to James' ears, it was a good half hour before James reluctantly volunteered to press on.

Fortunately, the rain had stopped. Removing their wet weather gear, they started off again.

They eventually arrived in Cheviot, surprisingly with no further moans from James. Established in the 1890s, the town was first known as McKenzie but later changed to Cheviot, referring to the Cheviot Hills that separate England from Scotland.

They managed to find a camp site just past the township where they were able to spread out some of the wet gear from the previous day's rain to dry in the sunshine.

Again, another longer bike ride the next day, to Greta Valley. This is almost the halfway point between Kaikoura and Christchurch. With well-dried wet-weather gear, they packed their backpacks and rode off to their new destination. Greta Valley is a small settlement named after the River Greta in Yorkshire, England.

They were surprised of the scenic openness compared to the heavier roadside vegetation earlier in their journey. James was just about to start his moaning again when Aroha stopped him in his tracks.

"Don't you utter a single word complaining of tiredness, or sore joints, or headache, etc, etc."

"I wasn't going to," said James, "well, not too much. I was just going to say when I save up enough money, I'm going to buy an electric bike, then I'll be so quiet you won't even know I'm here."

"Well, if that's the case, maybe I'll buy the bike for you," replied Aroha.

They had to travel a little distance past the settlement before they could locate a suitable camp site. On the way, however, they noticed a turnoff to Greta Valley School on Motunau Beach Road where a road sign indicated Motunau Beach, sixty kilometres. It was too far for them to deviate so they decided to stay on the highway.

Just over one kilometre off the coast lies Motunau Island. The island is a wildlife refuge that is home to white-flippered penguins and a variety of sea birds. Fur seals are also resident on the island.

Another thirty-kilometre bike ride, they chose to ride to Amberley. They didn't get too far when they had to stop for road works.

"Thank goodness, we can have a rest," said James.

"We've only biked for about five minutes," replied Aroha. "It's not going to be one of those days again."

"I can't help it if I tire easily," said James.

Finally, they were allowed to move on. It didn't take too long for the vehicles to pass them; they found themselves to be the only ones along the stretch of a one-lane road.

"This is quite a length of road works," said Aroha, "we had better cycle a bit faster so we don't hold up the traffic." They biked as fast as the uneven road surface would allow them. Eventually, they got to the works' end. The lollipop man had his hands on his hips, tapping the road with his left foot.

"We went as fast as we could," said Aroha.

The man smiled and said he was only joking. They make allowances for slower traffic.

"Travel safe," he called out, they waved and carried on their journey.

Biking past a turn off to State highway 7 the Weka Pass and Lewis Pass will lead you to Greym……

Amberley is a small town servicing the farming industry. A statue of Charles Upham, a highly decorated soldier of the Second World War is located in the centre of the township. In close proximity of the statue is a sculpture depicting 'The Three Grandmothers'. Carved from limestone, the sculpture represents the ancient peoples known as Waitaha.

The next stop is Woodend, a small town only twenty-five kilometres north of Christchurch City. The Waimakariri and Ashley rivers flow on either side of the town.

That evening, Aroha and James did a tally up of the little money they had left. "We are going to have to find employment pretty soon," said Aroha, "otherwise, we will totally run out of food. Probably look for a job in Ashburton, it's still quite a way off but I think we should last out till then."

"I hope we do last out," said James, "I get really hungry really quickly."

They didn't get too far, only about five kilometres. They decided to set up camp close to a wildlife reserve. Thinking that the closer they got to Kaiapoi, the more built-up it would become, making it difficult to camp. Also, their next stop was a campsite in Rolleston which was about forty kilometres, so best to have a bit of a rest before such a long trip.

Chapter 13
-43.531551,172.639642

The reserve is within the Kaiapoi area, only three kilometres from the Kaiapoi (Te Kōhaka -a-Kaikai-a-Waro) settlement. A significant pā site was established by the Māori chief Tūrakautahi. The name of the settlement was later shortened to Kaiapoi.

A slight northerly breeze was on their side, assisting their ride to Rolleston. They stayed on Main Road as cycling was not allowed on the Christchurch Motorway which forms part of State Highway 1. Crossing the Waimakariri River was somewhat scary as there was not very much room on the bridge with some vehicles passing at speed. Keeping extremely focused, they finally came to the end of it.

Main Road eventually met up with State Highway 1. Crossing the city was a monumental task; traffic was meeting them from all directions. Christchurch (Ōtautahi) is the country's second largest city receiving city status in 1856. Archaeological findings show that people inhabited Christchurch some eight hundred years ago.

The city layout includes a central city square surrounded by four smaller squares and parklands through its centre. The layout is based on similar designs established in the USA and Australia. Its geographic location puts Christchurch Airport in a perfect position to transporting passengers and equipment to Antarctica. Mainly for scientific research at the McMurdo and Scott bases.

Lyttleton Port, opened in 1877 is the major sea port of Christchurch. The harbour is some thirteen kilometres from the city. As well as a major shipping container port importing and exporting goods, cruise ships berth at the Lyttleton harbour.

On, they journeyed.

If you bear right onto state highway 73 it will get you to the other side through a pass Arthu……

They arrived in Rolleston for late lunch.

"Thank goodness," said James, "something to eat." Rolleston (Roretana, Tauwharekākaho) is in the Selwyn District. With its early beginnings as a rail terminus in 1866, it has evolved its railway network across to Greymouth on the West Coast, now taking passengers on the TranzAlpine Train.

After lunch, they headed off to look for lodging. Stopping at a travel centre, they enquired about camping ground facilities. On a map, the travel guide showed them the nearest camp area. With that, they rode off to find a suitable site. They were allowed to use the facilities at the camp; a welcomed treat to use the warm shower.

Aroha struck up a friendship with Polly, about the same age as Aroha, the daughter of the camp ground manager.

"So where have you come from?" enquired Polly.

"All the way from Cape Reinga," replied Aroha. "James and I have biked all the way except for a couple of short journeys by vehicle and the ferry crossing."

"Cool!" said Polly. "I wish I could do that; it would be awesome to visit all the places you have been to. Come on, I'll show you around the grounds. Oh, what about James?"

"He's OK," said Aroha, "we'll leave him to put up the tents."

Yep, you've guessed it, folks — grumble, grumble, grumble and on he went, questioning why he had to stay behind and do ALL the work whilst Aroha took a stroll with Polly.

"How long have you lived here?" asked Aroha.

"About five years," replied Polly. "It is quite fun, really, meeting lots of people from around New Zealand and overseas tourists. When I'm older," Polly continued, "I'm going to travel, probably first around New Zealand on a discovery expedition of my iwi (tribe) and cultural roots and then spend time overseas."

"That sounds great," said Aroha. "For some reason, I would like to go to Europe; so many countries and many different languages."

"My first adventure after New Zealand would be South America and the Amazon," said Polly, "to see Amazon wildlife in the flesh would be just awesome."

"Well," said Aroha, "maybe we might get back together one day in the future, explore our cultural roots and continue on a similar-type travel as James and I are doing here, but through Europe and the Amazon."

"Sounds like an excellent idea, I can't wait," replied Polly.

"I think we had better get back to our site," said Aroha, "otherwise, I won't hear the end of it from James."

Polly laughed. "I bet you two get on pretty well."

"Yes, we do really," said Aroha. "He gets to be a bit of a pain sometimes, but he's really good company."

They arrived back. "Well, it's nice that you have decided to come back," said James. "In the meantime, I have been slaving away here, WORKING!"

"See what I mean?" Aroha said as she turned to Polly.

"Yes, I do," replied Polly. "Have fun, see you tomorrow."

Next day, Aroha met up with Polly.

"So where to today?" asked Polly.

"Wanting to get to Rakaia," replied Aroha, "about thirty-five kilometres, and then on to Ashburton."

"Well, you be careful over the Rakaia Bridge," Polly advised, "it's quite long and doesn't have too much room for cyclists."

"We'll be careful," replied Aroha, and with that, she and James set off.

"Keep in touch," Polly called as she waved them on.

"We will," Aroha replied.

Only about five kilometres down the road, they noticed Burnham Military Camp signposted. Burnham is well-known for its defence force base. In the main, the base provides for medical training for all of the country's defence force.

On they pressed, their destination Rakaia, about thirty-six kilometres. They travelled along Brookside Road, then Selwyn Road and onto Rakaia Selwyn Road. They had to keep off the express way on State Highway 1. A large section of Brookside Road was gravel.

"This is a bit hard biking," said Aroha.

"Not for me," replied James; speeding up then jamming hard his back brake, skidding in the gravel.

"James, stop that!" exclaimed Aroha. "You'll fall off, and you'll wear out the tyre and get another puncture."

"Oops, didn't think of that," said James.

Only another couple of kilometres and they were back on the sealed road.

Eventually on State Highway 1 again and onto Main South Road; and there it was. In the distance, they could see the guard rail depicting the start of the longest bridge in New Zealand. Rakaia River Bridge which was opened in 1939 spans some 1,757 metres.

A daunting task, very little room on either side made this part of the trip a little scary. "I think if we just keep on top of the white side line," said Aroha, "at least it will keep us from straying too far into the traffic."

In single file, they rode nervously, keeping on or slightly within the white line as much as possible. With an extra burst of pedal power, they reached the end of the bridge. At last, a wide road shoulder made for less stressful cycling. They were going to have a rest on the side of the road after that harrowing ordeal but came to a road sign indicating a camping ground only a further two hundred metres, so decided to carry on, pitch their tents and have a well-deserved relaxing afternoon.

Rakaia lies within the Canterbury Plains. The 'Welcome to Rakaia' sign incorporates a large statue of a salmon. The Rakaia River flows close to the township. It is famously known for its salmon fishing.

Whilst an overcast but mild morning, the pair set off for Ashburton. Again, they had to leave State Highway 1 and travel along Dromore Hatfield Road for most of the journey. The last few kilometres brought them back onto the State Highway. Aroha turned to look behind her and saw that James was a long way behind, stopped on the side of the road.

What is he up to now? she thought. She turned back to see if he was all right.

"What are you up to?" she called.

"I found this," he waved a black pouch thing. "It's a wallet," he said, "I saw it lying in the grass."

"Is there anything in it?" asked Aroha.

"Yeeeees," James replied, looking in the wallet, then at Aroha, looking in the wallet again and again at Aroha. "There's lots of money."

"Let me have a look," said Aroha. She took out the money and counted $375. There were no other identification documents, just the money. Looking at each other, they found themselves in a bit of a dilemma. They could keep it, that would be a great help to them as they wouldn't need to find any employment. OR, they could take it to the police. After some vigorous debate, they reluctantly agreed to take it to the police. The police station was in the middle of the township.

"You don't think they'll know we have escaped the orphanage and handcuff us and take us back?" asked James.

"Hmmm, I don't know," said Aroha. "I hope they don't ask too many questions."

Cautiously, they entered the building and walked over to the enquiries desk. The receptionist (a lovely lady) helped them with their enquiry.

"You are very honest," she said. "Someone might be at their wits' end looking for it."

Aroha filled out the form and she had to include her name and address. Aroha and James waited nervously whilst the receptionist read through the details. "You are a long way from home," she said.

"Yes," Aroha replied, "visiting relatives," her voice breaking into a nervous stutter as she didn't like being dishonest even if it was a little white lie.

"We require all this information," the receptionist said, "if after a certain period of time the money is not claimed, then it can be returned to the person that found it — YOU."

Aroha and James thanked her and quickly exited the building before anyone became suspicious.

"I hope the money is not claimed," said James.

Now to look for some work. Not too far from the centre of town, they noticed a large building indicating an apiary.

"What about in there?" said James.

"I don't think so," said Aroha. "Do you remember when I was chased by a swarm of bees just out of Pukenui? I don't want that to happen again."

"We might get some other work, not necessarily working with bees," replied James.

They went inside to enquire.

Inside, there was a real hive (*Get it? Hive*) of activity, with wax being scraped, honey extracted and being filtered, bottling, packing and heaps more. The operations manager, Irene, asked them what they wanted and that they should have reported to reception rather than stroll into the main operations area.

"Sorry about that," said Aroha, "we got a bit lost. We are looking for a job for a few days."

"Well, I do as a matter of fact have something for you to do." She took them around the back of the main building and into a store shed. Hundreds of wooden hives just been put together.

"What are you like at painting?" she asked.

"Pretty good," said James, "we've done lots of painting."

Aroha looked at James but not letting on that they hadn't even held a paint brush.

"How long are you here for?" asked Irene.

"Probably four days," replied Aroha.

"Well, that's good." Irene went on, "If you are happy to do some painting, you can have a go at that lot. The paint is kept in the cupboard and next to that you'll find brushes and cleaning rags. If you spread out here along the work benches, you need to spread out the drop cloths over the floor and benches in case you spill any paint."

They were shown where to put the finished hives.

"I'll come back in a couple of hours to see how you are getting on."

"I would have preferred to work in the processing factory than smelling the paint fumes all day," said James.

"I agree," Aroha replied, "but we are only here for a short while just to make enough money for the rest of our journey."

"You're doing well," said Irene, inspecting the paint work of the finished hives as she walked in.

"It's nearly five, so you may as well finish up, clean the brushes and I'll see you tomorrow morning at eight."

"Would it be okay if we could stay in one of your buildings overnight rather than going to a camping ground?" asked Aroha.

"I think that should be fine," said Irene, "you can stay in the workers' quarters as they are not being used this week. Do you have sleeping bags?" she asked.

"Yes," replied James, "we have all our own gear."

For the next few days, it was white paint, and more white paint. "How many hives do you think we've painted?" asked Aroha.

"I have no idea," replied James, "I stopped counting after the first million."

"I think you're exaggerating a bit once again," said Aroha.

At the end of the fourth day, Irene came in to see Aroha and James and commented on how neatly they had painted the hives. Giving them their wages, she wished them well on their journey.

Ashburton (Hakatere) is a farming district. A grand scale irrigation system was developed between 1937 and 1944 from the Rangitata River. The system, the largest in the country, can irrigate over a hundred thousand hectares of pasture. In addition to land irrigation, it provides water for two hydroelectric power stations and a stock water race system.

On they rode through Ealing.

By turning right onto state highway 77 and then 73, you will end up at Kum... Jun.....

They passed a sign directing to Peel Forest. A campsite managed by the Conservation Department. Peel Forest is a remnant of a large forest which amongst other native flora includes significant stands of rimu, kahikatea, miro, matai and tōtara trees. One main feature, a tōtara, is estimated to be a thousand years old. A bit off the beaten track, they decided to stay at the campsite. Such a beautiful area, covered in native trees and close to the Rangitata River.

A very fine drizzle welcomed them the next day. On with the wet weather gear again, although they had been fortunate with the mainly fine weather so far throughout the journey. Fortunately, not too much traffic for Sunday morning. The wet road made for a slippery surface.

"Ride carefully," called Aroha.

"I will," answered James.

They biked around a fairly sharp bend which carried on for some distance before straightening itself out to the long straights they had been used to for the last few days. Suddenly, a small car came around the corner at a speed certainly not consistent with the road conditions. It managed to get itself into a skid, narrowly missing Aroha and James and ended up in the roadside water table before hitting a seven-wire fence.

Aroha and James hurried over to the car. An elderly couple were trying to free themselves from their seatbelts, struggling to get out of the car. Aroha took charge.

"Please don't move," she said to the driver, "my name is Aroha, just wanting to check that you are not injured."

"I'm all right," he said, "but check my wife."

Aroha went across to the passenger side and saw that the elderly lady had a deep laceration to her forearm. "I'll just go and get something." Digging deep into her backpack, Aroha pulled out a small first aid kit. She used some alcohol-based preps to clean the wound, placing a sterile dressing covering the cut. She then bound it with a crepe bandage.

"You might like to keep your arm raised to help stop the bleeding," she suggested.

"I don't know what I would have done without you," said the lady.

Meanwhile, James waved down a motorist and asked if they could call for an ambulance.

"We don't need an ambulance, we are both fine," said the elderly man.

The motorist wouldn't hear of it and dialled 111. The elderly man was suddenly overcome by shivering and became a little disorientated. Helping him back into the driver's seat, Aroha looked in the back of the car. Finding a rug, she and the motorist put it over the elderly man and found a coat that they put over the injured lady. It wasn't too long that they heard a siren in the distance; help was on its way. It was a police car that appeared around the corner, followed closely by an ambulance. As the medics took over, they remarked how well Aroha had cared for the couple and placing a rug over the man was the right thing to do as he was entering a state of shock despite not being injured.

With that, Aroha and James wished the couple well, thanked the motorist and continued their journey.

"That was a bit of an experience," said James.

"Yes," agreed Aroha. "I have never been at a car crash before, just as well I had a first aid kit."

They decided to stay at a campsite in Temuka, mainly for the fact that riding in the drizzly rain made them cold and wet and also attending at the crash site, a hot shower would be a very welcome treat.

Temuka is famous for its stoneware creations where pottery had been established in the 1930s and still continues today to meet the high demands for these products.

Chapter 14
-44.396958,171.256145

Next morning, they made use of the camp ground's facilities; able to wash and dry clothes and spread tents and sleeping gear out in the sunshine. They didn't need to journey too early as their next stop Timaru was only eighteen kilometres. It wasn't until close to lunchtime that they set off and decided to have a lunch break at the next rest area.

They eventually arrived in Timaru and decided to bike a little past the township to set up camp and bike back for a look around. Timaru, originally spelt Te Maru (the Shelter), established a large port on reclaimed land. Hills around the area were made from lava that was spewed from the volcano known as Mount Horrible (the story goes that a surveyor whilst surveying the mount had a horrible day, hence its name) that last erupted some two million years ago. Bluestone used for building and decorative purposes is quarried from the lava tracts. The volcano is now extinct. Māori rock art can be seen in the Opuha and Opihi valleys within the Temuka district.

The next stretch was a fifty-two-kilometre journey to Morven. They thought they would make up for the short distance travelled the previous day. Surprisingly, it was James that suggested the longer trip; it remains to be seen whether or not there will be moans and groans along the way.

Not a peep out of him. "Are you feeling OK, James?" asked Aroha.

"Yes," replied James, "why do you ask?"

"Well, we are nearly at Morven, travelled over fifty kilometres and I haven't heard any groans from you."

"Ha ha, very funny," said James, "I have built-in stamina, I can bike for ages."

Aroha just rolled her eyes. They decided to set up camp in Morven. They thought about going to the Waimate township but being a further eight kilometres off the main road, they decided to call it a day.

Waimate is known for its white horse landmark which is situated in Centrewood Park. It is a large structure of a Clydesdale horse made of concrete paving stones. It represents the Clydesdale horses that were used in the early days of the town's development.

The bush areas not far from the township are home to the Bennetts Wallabies, imported from Australia in 1874 for their fur trade and sport. The population has significantly increased, causing damage to the native environment.

Next morning, they set off for Oamaru. As they travelled, James was a little concerned about Aroha. She hardly spoke, her sad demeanour was uncharacteristic, so much so that James had to say something.

"Are you OK?" asked James. "You don't look your usual self."

"I'm OK," said Aroha mournfully. "No, I'm not," she admitted.

"What's the matter?" asked James.

They stopped in a wide area off the road, and Aroha sat beside a large pine tree.

"Do you ever wonder who your parents might be?"

"Now and again, but not very often," replied James.

"Sometimes, I wish I knew," Aroha said in a soft voice. "I don't even know which iwi I belong to." Tears started rolling down her cheeks.

James put his arm around her to offer some comfort.

"I'm just being silly," Aroha went on.

"No, you're not, I suppose in your culture it is quite important to know your heritage," replied James. "I suppose," he went on, "there is a need in everyone to know where they belong, I just don't think about it too much as despite how I dislike old baggy pants matron at the orphanage, I do have quite a few friends there. Don't forget, you became good friends with Polly. Wouldn't it be a good idea if you joined her on the iwi and cultural adventure she wants to go on?" Aroha nodded. "Plus, you have meeeeeeeeeeeeee."

Aroha laughed at his mildly funny antics.

"You are a good friend," she said. With that, they rode on.

At last, they arrived in Oamaru (Te Oha-a-Maru — the place of Maru) which was first settled by Europeans in 1853. Famously known for limestone mining, the product is known as Oamaru Stone. It is used not only as a building material but ideal for carving and sculptures.

The Steampunk (futuristic science fiction combined with steam-powered machinery of the 19 century) Capital of New Zealand is Oamaru. The first festival began in 2009 and is held annually. In 2016, the Guinness Book of World Records promoted Oamaru for the largest gathering of Steampunks.

The next stop is the small township of Herbert (renamed from Otepopo). They decided to stay the night at a camping ground a couple of kilometres south of the township. A beautiful setting of trees and shrubs and bounded by the Waianakarua River. With deep swimming holes, James was the first to take the plunge followed closely by Aroha.

"I could live here forever," said James, looking up at the clear sky whilst negotiating the back-stroke. After some more swimming and races, which James failed at miserably, they had a wander around the grounds before settling in for the evening.

The following morning was a trip to Shag Point (Matakaea) that consisted of a rugged coastline. The largest dinosaur fossil was found in the area; a Plesiosaur estimated at seventy million years old. With a length of seven metres, it is the largest dinosaur fossil found in New Zealand and is housed in the Otago Museum. They decided to travel a further ten kilometres and stop for a break at a rest area. They came to a sign indicating Moeraki Boulders Car Park. Thinking that a good place to rest, they biked over to the beach.

"Look at those boulders!" exclaimed James.

"What an awesome sight!" replied Aroha. They ventured closer to the rocks. What an unusual sight, large round boulders ranging in size between half a metre to over two metres in diameter. Strewn along the beach, they have become a tourist attraction.

Chapter 15
-45.873465,170.503605

Next day, they decided to head to Merton some thirty kilometres and then a similar distance to Dunedin. Whilst two fairly lengthy journeys, they agreed to stay in Dunedin a couple of nights. Just nine kilometres from Shag Point, they passed through Palmerston. The flat land around Palmerston gives rise to the striking landmark of Puketapu (Sacred Hill).

By turning onto state highway 85 you will eventually get to Alex.....

Passing through Goodwood, Flag Swamp, and Waikouaiti, they arrived in Merton, a farming locality. Rows of tree shelter belts by the roadside made for suitable secluded campsites.

The early morning rise focussed on their trip to Dunedin.

"I'm excited about going to Dunedin," said James.

"And what is it about Dunedin that has brought this on?" asked Aroha.

"Not too sure," replied James, "I have read a bit about it and sounds like a cool place. One of my friends at the orphanage is from Dunedin and he keeps talking about the albatross colony but can't remember too much about it."

"Albatross colony?" Aroha exclaimed. "Wow! I'd love to see them."

The first settlement they passed was Warrington (Okahau). One of only a few left in the world, a Futuro house built in the 1970s still stands in Warrington. The house designed by Finnish architect Matti Suuronen had only a hundred built in several countries during the 1960s and 1970s. The building is in the shape of a UFO made from fibreglass-reinforced polyester plastic. The eight-metre-wide dwelling stands on stilt legs where a hatch with steps opens out for access.

Cycling through Evansdale and Waitati, the road started to get hillier.

"I'm pooped," said James, "these hills are getting too much."

Aroha agreed. "We'll stop at the next rest area for lunch and a bit of a break."

After lunch, they made another assault on the hilly terrain.

"I can't pedal any further," said Aroha, "I think it would be easier to walk some of the way."

James didn't hesitate, he hopped off his bike and followed Aroha. "I wonder how long this goes for," said James, "I hope it's not all the way to Dunedin."

Well, it was a few kilometres by foot, they managed to cycle a few metres where the road seemed to plateau a little and then back on foot again. They calculated five to six kilometres for the steepest parts, eventually reaching the crest.

"I think it's downhill from here to Dunedin," said Aroha.

"Thank goodness for that!" replied James.

Down they raced along the beautiful, scenic Leith Valley, and eventually the city of Dunedin.

Not far from the town centre is a holiday park with camping ground facilities. They decided to spend two nights at the grounds to have a bit of a look around the city and a break from cycling. "I can't wait to see the albatross," said Aroha, "let's go to the information centre and make some enquiries."

At the centre, they were shown a map of the road and nature reserve at Taiaroa Head. The options to get there were taxi or bus; neither of which they could afford. The only other option was to bike there, problem was the thirty-three-kilometre distance there and back. They both looked somewhat forlorn.

"Well, we might have to forgo the albatross this time," said Aroha. "One day, if we ever make it back to Dunedin, hopefully we might get the opportunity to see them."

They didn't notice a person standing close by as they were discussing their tale of woe.

"Hi," came a voice from behind. "I couldn't help overhearing that you have no way of getting to the albatross colony."

Aroha turned to the lady in a green top with Department of Conservation (DOC) logo.

"Hello," said Aroha, "we would love to see the albatross but it's too expensive for us and a bit too far to cycle."

"My name is Emily. I am a DOC Ranger and I am going out there just for an hour. I'll give you a ride if you like?"

"That would be SUPER!" said James. "My name is James and this is Aroha."

"Pleased to meet you," said Emily, "just give me a few minutes to get some gear." She pointed to a DOC ute. "If you wait next to the ute for me, I'll be over shortly."

Excitedly, they waited impatiently for Emily. "OK, hop in," she said.

"This is very nice of you," said Aroha.

"It would have been a shame for you to miss out on such an awesome experience," said Emily. "I can only take you to the visitor centre," she continued, "only authorised staff can enter the colony."

"That would be excellent," said Aroha. "Hopefully, there will be an albatross to see."

It didn't take very long when they arrived at the visitor centre. "I'll drop you off here," said Emily, "and will pick you up in about an hour."

They would have liked to go further to the viewing area but were content with being at the centre and hopefully might just get a glimpse. It was quite a windy day. James commented on the wind saying how pleased he was not to have to bike in the wind.

"Look, look up there," said Aroha. There gliding in the breeze was this magnificent bird. "Just look at it," said Aroha, "isn't this just fantastic?"

James agreed, as he pointed to two other albatrosses further away. They gazed into the sky in awe for the next quarter hour.

Taiaroa Head is located at the end of the Otago Peninsula. The area is named after the Māori chief Te Mātenga Taiaroa. Over a hundred northern royal albatross nest in the reserve. The Department of Conservation manage the nature reserve with the Otago Peninsula Trust managing the visitor centre. A sheltered spot near the albatross centre is an area known as Pilots Beach. A number of seals, blue penguins and yellow-eyed penguins have made it their breeding habitat.

Emily arrived after about an hour, picked up Aroha and James and took them back to the information centre where the pair had left their bikes.

"Well, did you see any?" she asked.

"Yes, thanks to you," said James. Three of them were circling above.

"You are lucky that it is quite windy today," Emily continued, "albatross take advantage of the wind currents which help them to glide gracefully around the Reserve area."

They thanked Emily and headed to the campground.

Next day was a tour around Dunedin, marvelling at the sight of grand old stone buildings.

"Isn't there a street where they roll round Jaffa sweets in Dunedin?" asked James.

"Not sure," replied Aroha, "maybe we can ask someone."

They went into a dairy and whilst buying a chocolate bar each, asked the proprietor.

"Oh yes," he said, "it's Baldwin Street, just three kilometres from the city centre. You know it was officially recognised as the world's steepest street by the Guinness Book of Records. It all started in 2001 and ever since each July, some seventy-five thousand jaffas (a small round chocolate sweet with a hard covering) are rolled from the top of the hill. A competitor is allocated a number which is attached to the jaffa sweet. They are sold for a $1 each, proceeds of which go to charity. There are prizes for the winners."

He gave them directions and they set off to this world-renowned street. "I'm not even going to attempt to bike up it," said Aroha.

"Nor me," replied James. "Let's just push our bikes up."

Eventually at the top, they ate their well-earned chocolate bars.

"Last one to the bottom is a dumpling," said James.

"Hold on, hold on," replied Aroha, "just take it slowly and keep your brakes on. You just wouldn't be able to stop if you went too fast."

James took Aroha's advice and they cautiously rode down the street. "Well, that was quite an experience," said Aroha. "The world's steepest street, and we've been on it."

Next day, they set off leaving the city and back into the rural environment.

They chose to camp outside of Henley, the town hosts a number of rowing events on Lake Waihola. Biking through Waihola, the panoramic views of Lake Waihola and the surrounding wetlands are breathtaking. The significant wetland area is home to over ten thousand water fowl. Native plants are continually planted in and around the wetlands by a dedicated army of volunteers.

They decided to stop for lunch in Milburn. Just entering Milburn, a road sign indicated a lime works.

"I have heard something about the relevance of the lime works," said Aroha, "but I can't remember what it was."

"Let's go and take a look," suggested James.

They biked for about three kilometres and came to the lime works, but other than a large excavation site, there was nothing much to be seen. Just then, one of the quarry workers came cycling by. Aroha asked him if there is a place of interest close by. He told her there is the Milburn lookout about one kilometre up the road. They rode off and came to some large rocks arranged on the side of the road with a gate between them.

"I think it might be through the gate," said Aroha.

Through the gate, they were greeted by a building. They walked over to the lookout point where they had a fantastic view of Lake Waihola and farmland. Returning back, they entered the building which to their surprise housed a display of whale and dolphin fossils that were found in the nearby lime quarries. The fossils are estimated at between 24—34 million years old.

"That's pretty old," said James.

"Absolutely fascinating," replied Aroha.

Biking back, they ended at their destination for the day in Milton (formally known as Tokomairiro). Milton's initial growth was supported by the gold prospecting era of the 1860s.

Aroha and James decided to spend the night at a camp ground close by. They were being watched by an elderly couple at the next site. As soon as they had erected their tents, Bob (the husband) who was watching them set up camp called out to them "Would you like a nice, cooked meal?" whilst keeping an eye on the food sizzling on his extraordinarily large barbeque.

"That would be fantastic!" replied James as he walked over to see what was cooking.

"I'm James, and that's Aroha still finishing erecting her tent."

"Pleased to meet you, James. I'm Bob and my wife still making a salad is Mabel. Well," said Bob, "we have sausages, bacon, chicken wings, potatoes, onions and salad, so I hope you are hungry."

"You bet," replied James.

Three girls came over who were from the next tent site and were also invited to the feast. Aroha came to join them all.

Bob started by saying he often cooks up a large meal with the help of his wife and they generally invite camp neighbours as they tour the country-side. It is a good way to meet people and share travel experiences. The girls were from Scotland on their big OE, had landed in Christchurch and were travelling by a hired car down to Bluff and up the West Coast and then on to the North Island. When Aroha entered the conversation that they have biked from Cape Reinga, everyone was astounded at the huge distance the pair had accomplished.

"We are also going down to Bluff," Aroha continued, "and then hopefully up the West Coast."

James' face said it all. "Bike the West Coast?"

"Yes," said Aroha, "might as well make the most of it, the scenery is reputed to be magnificent."

"Well, we wish you luck," said Mabel, "that's a huge journey."

Can I fit in one more sausage? James thought to himself, after finishing his fourth. *Yes, I'm sure I can, one can never tell this could be my last meal for a very long time,* he convinced himself.

"Eat up, eat up," said Mabel.

James took one sausage. Mabel put another in his hand.

"I can't—"

"Nonsense," said Mabel, "you eat up, you'll need it for your next excursion."

"We will need to turn in," said Aroha. "Need to start early in the morning."

They thanked the hosts and bid the three travellers goodnight. Next morning, they set off before anyone else decided to get up.

Biking through Balclutha township, they came across a huge bridge structure over the Clutha River. Whilst the roadway is fairly narrow, the bridge has a cycleway/pedestrian access. Balclutha (Iwikatea) is a major service centre for the surrounding agriculture industry. They biked a short distance from the town where they could set up camp for the night.

The following day, they decided to stay on State Highway 1 and headed to Clinton. They did think about travelling south on Southern Scenic Highway which would have led them to the Catlins reserve but agreed it would be too far to detour off the main route.

The Catlins whilst it covers a significant land area is sparsely populated with about one thousand residents. It is a nature paradise where heavy forested areas meet sandy beaches. The rugged coastline extends out to the cave systems which includes the famous Cathedral Caves. Large expanses of wetland are home to an array of water fowl and mammals. If you wander further inland, you can view a number of waterfalls, as they cascade down the rock shelves. In low-tide at Curio Bay, you can view the fossilised remains of a Jurassic forest some one hundred and eighty million years old. It has become an internationally important scientific site.

They stopped at Clinton for a break and overnight stay. Rather than take a short cut along Highway 93 which joins up with Highway 1, they decided to stay on State Highway 1 to visit Gore. Being a forty-kilometre trip, they set off early but had a few breaks on the way. Having lunch at a rest area, James began.

"Are we really going to bike along the West Coast back home?"

"I think we should," replied Aroha. "It would be awesome to see the other side of the country. Wouldn't you want another adventure, plus there is nothing really to go to at the orphanage."

"Yes, it would be great," agreed James, "but maybe we should rest up for a week or so before we set off."

"Oh yes, we will need to," said Aroha. "We would also need to find employment to pay for camp sites and food as we have done for the east coast adventure. We are running out of money but I think we have enough to see us through to Bluff."

They decided to live it up in Gore and stay at a camping ground; a treat for biking over forty kilometres. Gore (Maruawai) with the Mataura River known for its Brown Trout fishing runs through the township. Gore has a sister city relationship with the city of Tamworth in New South Wales, Australia. The relationship hinges around Country and Western music. With Gore holding its annual event the New Zealand

Gold Guitars Awards, and Tamworth its annual Country Music Festival has made it a perfect choice for this relationship between the two communities.

If you turn right onto state highway 94 you will eventually join with highway 6. Highway 94 terminates at Milford Sound whilst northward bound on highway 6 passes through the playground of the South Island known as Queens……

Chapter 16
-46.417678,168.361481

Next, it was on to Edendale. During its early settlement, it was also known as Maorirua, Mataura Plains and Stuart's Bush. Of note is the large dairy manufacturing plant. Its origins indicate it was the first dairy factory in New Zealand. The plant has expanded many times over the years and in 2009 made it the largest milk processing site in the world.

They were on the road again with Invercargill in their sights.

"Look at that!" said Aroha. "Come on."

Following her, James looked to the sky, to the ground, left and right. "What am I supposed to be looking at?" he called.

Aroha had already climbed over the fence. "Just look, isn't it amazing?"

"I really don't know what you are looking at," said James.

"Can't you see them, millions and millions of daisies?"

James rolled his eyes. "So what?" he said.

"Aren't they just beautiful!" exclaimed Aroha.

"Very lovely," said James with a bit of a sigh.

"Come on," said Aroha, "lie down on the bed of daisies."

James obediently followed suit.

"Isn't this just awesome?" said Aroha. A mass of white daises for as far as the eye could see. James did tend to agree with her. Staring up into the sky, Aroha reminisced what might be going on at the orphanage; and did any of the other children decide to leave?

"It's the only home I know," she said, "if it weren't for ugly, bossy matron, it would be a nice place to live."

"Yes, I miss the guys too," said James. "We did all have fun, when bossy breeches wasn't around."

"Look at the shapes those white fluffy woollen clouds are making, I can see a head of a horse," said Aroha.

"Yes, and the one next to it looks like a Viking with his horned helmet," replied James.

As they were chatting and day dreaming, Aroha was making daisy chains, ten in all.

"Have you got enough of those things?" asked James.

"I think this will do just nicely," said Aroha, five on each handlebar, but she did make a special one for James.

"Where am I going to put this?" he exclaimed.

"I'm sure you'll find somewhere on your bike," replied Aroha. "OK, time to go," she continued.
Invercargill (Waihōpai) is the southernmost city in New Zealand. Invercargill was the birth place of Burt Munro,

the motorcycle racer who set a world record for under 1,000 cc motorcycle at two hundred and ninety five kilometres an hour on the salt flats in Bonneville USA. The world record still stands today.

The Invercargill March is a famous musical march for brass band. It was composed by Alex Lithgow who lived in Invercargill. The famous march is played the world over.

Biking through the city, they rode a couple of kilometres into the rural area where they set up camp.

"Well, I suppose heading to Bluff will be our last journey on the east coast," said James. "Will be a bit sad coming to the end of the line, all the fun and sights we have had and seen; it has been awesome."

Aroha agreed, and yes, there was a sense of finality to the adventure even though they had agreed to continue up the western side of the country.

Eventually, they turned in for the night, wanting to get as much rest as possible for the final leg of their journey. It was about eleven thirty p.m. and James just could not get to sleep. Tossing and turning and really quite wide awake. He shut his eyes tight, tried to dismiss any thoughts, breathing slowly and deeply, but no; he was so wide awake that he could have even biked to Bluff there and then. He rolled outside of his tent and thought he would go for a stroll. He stood motionless and in awe looking up in the night sky. With nervous excitement, he went over to Aroha's tent.

"Are you awake?" he said in a loud whisper. "Aroha, are you awake" he repeated.

"Mmmm, what do you want, I'm asleep," came the response.

"Quick, come outside and have a look at this," his whisper got louder.

Aroha crawled out of her tent, her eyes partially closed. "Can't you see I'm asleep; this had better be good."

"Look up there," said James.

Aroha looked up, rubbed her eyes and looked again; her fixed gaze rendered her body motionless just as it had affected James. The Southern Lights (Aurora Australis). The green and pink hue of the aurora dancing over the horizon lighting up the sky. It was a perfect night to see the lights as the sky was clear, there was no moon, and they were far enough from the city's light pollution.

Auroras are electrically charged solar particles. The combination of these particles with gases like oxygen and nitrogen emit various colours of light.

"See, what do you think?" said James.

"I wouldn't have missed this for the world," replied Aroha. They watched the aurora activity for at least an hour before going back to their tents; this time, it didn't take long for either of them to drop off into a deep sleep.

Aroha woke up with a start. Looking at her watch, ten thirty a.m.

"We've slept in," she said quite loudly, hoping for James to hear. "Are you getting up this morning?" she said to James who was fast asleep. She shook his shoulder. "We are going to be late, we are late, it is late, wake up!"

"What's the time?" mumbled James.

"Time you were up," Aroha replied. "We've slept in," she repeated.

Having downed breakfast in two minutes and packed up, they started for Bluff. Bluff (Motupōhue), earlier known as Port Macquarie and Campbelltown, is a sea port town. The deep-water port officially opened in 1960. Whilst Slope Point is actually the furthest south of the South Island mainland, Bluff is normally referred to as the southern extremity as the two end points of New Zealand are referred to as Cape Reinga to Bluff.

At Stirling Point at the end of State Highway 1, a directional signpost has been constructed showing distances to a number of locations around the world and including Cape Reinga.

Some forty kilometres south of Bluff across the Foveaux Strait lies Stewart Island. A large sculpture of an anchor chain has been constructed in Bluff. A similar structure by the shore of Stewart Island representing the other end of the chain. The sculpture is a symbol of the Māori belief of the joining of the two islands.

They came to a road sign indicating Greenpoint Track.

"Shall we have a look?" asked Aroha.

"Yes, I think we can. We have got plenty of time as we aren't too far from Bluff," replied James.

They came to a Heritage Trails sign titled 'Greenpoint Domain and Ship's Graveyard'. The pair looked at each other and then read on. It talks about the area as being home to a number of boat and ship wrecks. They walked a little further to a viewing platform where they could just make out part of the larger ships. The tide was going out but the best time to see them is at low tide.

They decided to stay at a camping ground as the intention was to stay in Bluff for a while. Next day, they biked to Stirling Point. The end of the line for State Highway 1. Bluff to Cape Reinga, where the adventure started, is one thousand four hundred kilometres although the actual road trip was a little over two thousand kilometres.

"That's quite an achievement," said James. "I never thought we would actually make it."

Aroha couldn't believe it either, the thought of cycling from one end of the country to the other.

They biked back to the camping ground where they were going to leave their bikes and walk into the township.

"There it is again," said James excitedly.

"What is?" asked Aroha.

"Wait there," James replied, "I'll be back soon."

He ran around the camping ground in and around tents, and motor homes, and caravans and people. It was ten minutes later that he emerged, the grin on his face from ear to ear.

He looked behind him. "Come on," he called.

"What's going on?" asked Aroha.

"I told you so, didn't I, on the ferry, I told you but you wouldn't believe me."

Out of the bush like a bullet, it raced and jumped up at Aroha, licking her face. "It's Timmy!" cried James. "Our long-lost friend, it's Timmy."

Aroha didn't know what had struck her, she was startled, excited, disbelieving at first. "Is it really you?"

Timmy jumped and ran around, wagging his tail. They were so pleased to see him.

"I don't know how but he must have followed us all this distance; and why wait until now to find us? Does he also think it's the end of the line?" asked James. "From now on," James continued, "I won't let you out of my sight, we are a threesome from this moment on."

"Let's all go for a walk into town," said Aroha. "It's just about lunchtime anyway."

The three travellers set off, with Timmy in the middle.

"Well, are we going to do it?" asked Aroha.

"Do what?" replied James.

"We are in Bluff," Aroha continued, "and what is famous in Bluff?"

"What?" asked James.

"Well, fresh oysters, of course," replied Aroha.

"I'm not having any of those," James insisted.

"I'm afraid you have no say in the matter," Aroha mused. There it was a sign said 'Fresh Oysters'.

"Come on," said Aroha, "we'll get one each."

They were shown how to eat them by the shop owner. "Just let it slide off the shell and straight in the mouth," he told them.

Aroha went first, closed her eyes and the facial expression turned into, *Wow, that tastes good.*

James reluctantly tried the same, then ran outside; he couldn't swallow it.

"Maybe if they were cooked, I would eat them," he said.

Chapter 18
-34.448146,172.704514

Well, at least they tried, but Aroha might have got a taste for them. Off they went, with Timmy close by.

"'Ello, 'ello, 'ello, what 'av' we 'ear then, eh?"

They turned around, as did Timmy. Two police constables were standing behind them. The man was built like a bus, they were straining their necks looking up at him, the lady reminded them of Matron at the orphanage. Timmy could have none of this; lying down, he put his paws over his eyes.

The policeman pulled out from his pocket a crinkled sheet of paper; looked at the paper, looked at the pair, looked at the paper, looked at the pair. Showed the paper to his colleague who looked at the paper and looked at the pair. They looked at each other and nodded in agreement.

"You two," he said, "are from the orphanage up north, aren't you?"

The pair didn't say anything, just nodded.

"You have been on the missing persons list for months, the staff at the orphanage are beside themselves worrying about your safety."

The pair looked at each other, unable to hide the look of guilt. Although both of them had this unusual thought that they just couldn't imagine Matron worrying about them, perhaps they had misjudged her.

The policewoman called through to the station that they have found the missing duo and their furry friend.

"Bring them back to the police station," was the response.

The three were ushered to the car's back seat and delivered to the station.

"Do you think they will put us in a jail cell?" James whispered to Aroha.

"I don't know," she replied.

They were escorted to a room and offered a can of soft drink (Timmy was also allowed in). "Well, how are we going to get you back home?" asked the policeman.

"We can always bike," replied James.

The policeman was not amused. Just then, another policeman came in.

"We have found a way to get you two home," he said.

They organised to take the pair (and their travelling buddy) back to the camping ground to pick up their gear and bikes. Then drove them to a large open space.

"Now, we wait," said the policeman.

Aroha and James looked at each other in bewilderment. *What's going on?* they thought.

A whirling sound was heard in the distance, gradually getting louder; until it was heard right above them.

"Just stay in the car," the driver said, "I'll tell you when it's safe to get out."

Landing right beside them was a brand-new police helicopter.

"I've always wanted a ride in a helicopter," said James. "I bet Timmy has too."

"The new helicopter was only received into the force yesterday," said the pilot, "and it's destined for Auckland."

They took all their belongings and made their way for embarking. "Be careful of the paint work with those bikes," said the pilot.

Loaded up, they were off. A fast vertical take-off and in seconds, the trees looked like tiny seedlings.

Despite the thrill of the helicopter ride, both Aroha and James felt a sense of sadness leaving their adventure and freedom behind. It wasn't too long in the journey that they were circling over the orphanage building.

"This is where it all started," said James.

"Yes," replied Aroha, "that was quite a long time ago."

As they were descending, they could make out figures on the ground. The closer they got, the better they could see that they were the children from the orphanage waving to them. Eventually landing and the rotors finally coming to a stop, the helicopter was surrounded by youngsters clambering over and under it, pressing for a closer look.

Aroha and James stepped out, there was a deafening hooray welcoming them back.

Jon came up to James, put his arm around him and said, "I am so gruntled they you are both back safe and sound."

Taking their belongings, they thanked the pilot and followed the gang back home. On arrival, they were met by an attractive middle-aged lady.

"Welcome home," she said. "We were very worried about your safety as you had been gone for such a long time."

"This is Miss Matilda Merry," said Jon, "our new matron who has been with us for three months. Matron Mayonnaise Spreadable has left. Also, the orphanage name has been changed from 'Broken Bones' to 'Funny Bones'."

Aroha and James were delighted to be back.

"Can we keep Timmy?" asked James. "I promise he will be looked-after, you won't even know he's here."

"Of course, you can, James," said Matilda. "It will be nice to have such a lovely pet as part of the family. Well, you get yourselves sorted out and cleaned up," said Matilda. "When you are done, I will make everyone a drink of hot chocolate and you can tell us all your adventures."

The stories flowed out of Aroha and James, it was close to midnight and they hadn't even scratched the surface of their tales.

"Time for bed," said Matilda, "we'll resume tomorrow after breakfast."

Next day, whilst they were having breakfast, there was a knock on the door.

"Who can that be at this early hour?" said Matilda. She came back with a sombre look. "It's the police and they want to talk with Aroha and James."

They went into another room, nervously awaiting a further dressing down by the arm of the law.

The police had left and Aroha and James came back into the dining room. All went quiet, *what was going to happen to Aroha and James?* Aroha explained that on their trip, they found a wallet containing $375, which they handed in at a police station. As no one had claimed the money, it was given back to the finders.

"So," said James, "we are going to use the money for the biggest party anyone has ever seen!"

Amidst the cheering and noise, Matilda suggested the party be held the following weekend so that all the arrangements could be made.

Aroha then spoke up, "How pleased we are to be back amongst all our friends and hope one day you too can experience the wonders of this beautiful country."

James added, "I have kept a diary of events that took place and what we have seen and I think I will call it Marco Polo the Second."

Matilda said, "That would be a nice title but, what you have described to us sounds like an amazing adventure all happening here in New Zealand (Aotearoa). So, what about Aotearoa An Amazing Adventure?"

"Perfect," said James, "that's exactly what it was, yes, that will be the title."

A story where fate led two children in the discovery of life events, diversity and an amazing encounter of New Zealand's cultural significance and natural beauty.